WHAT DA LICK READ?

Beastmode

PART 2

SEVYN MCCRAY

To my brother, Randy Jerome Menefee (B.K.A.) R.J. AKA Street Money Strike
July 24, 1978-January 26, 2014
I love you with all of me. May your memory live throughout eternity. "Cowards die many times before their deaths; The valiant never taste of death but once."

ACKNOWLEDGMENTS

TO EVERYONE WHO EVER BOUGHT A BOOK WRITTEN BY SEVYN MCCRAY, I love you and appreciate you from the bottom of my heart.

PLAYLIST

You will notice that many of the chapter titles are titles or verses of songs. Please enjoy this "What Da Lick Read? 2" inspired playlist on Apple Music.

https://music.apple.com/us/playlist/what-da-lick-read-2-beastmode/pl.u-pMylEAaHZxNN56

DEAR READER,

What's good, fam? If you're back for round two of 'What Da Lick Read?', thank you for riding with me again! And if this is your first time here—welcome! You're about to dive into something wild.

'What Da Lick Read?' Part 1 hit hard, thanks to your support. Now I'm bringing you the re-edited and updated sequel, Beastmode. It's bigger, bolder, and polished up with a fresh graphics and a playlist inspired by events. These characters are coming back stronger, with even more twists and betrayals.

Quick heads-up: this story is for your enjoyment but does contain sensitive subjects, which may be hard for some readers.

Thank you for your love and support—let's get back to these Atlanta streets!

Much love,
Sevyn McCray

PROLOGUE

-Perry Heights Atlanta, Georgia 1993

Everyone was asleep as she tiptoed barefoot into the kitchen to get some of her favorite soda, Tahitian Treat. She probably would have been home in bed if she hadn't been so mad at her sister. She wished Solitaire would get her shit together and come to get them. Beautiful wished she had an everyday life. But the last bit of normalcy seemed to have left her house on the day her Auntie Brilliant was found dead of a heart attack in her bedroom. Now, her grandmother was in the hospital suffering from her fourth stroke since her youngest daughter died, and Beautiful's siblings were lying in the apartment next door by themselves.

She heard loud footsteps on the hardwood floors as she closed the refrigerator. They were heavy, so she knew they could only belong to Big Man. Beautiful looked around the small kitchen; there was nowhere to hide from him. Ever since the first time he touched her, she had tried to stay out of his sight. She wanted to kick herself. She should've just stayed at home. Gorgeous bossing her around was nothing compared to what Big Man did to her. Her heart pounded in her chest as he walked into the kitchen. She wished she was like the little girl from her favorite television show, *Small Wonder,* and that she could freeze time. She would freeze it, run home, jump in the bed with her twin sister, start time back up, and close her eyes.

"I was a little thirsty myself," Big Man said as he stood in the doorway, his big eyes leering lustfully at Beautiful as she cowered in the corner by the refrigerator.

Her long jet-black hair hung down her back in a French braid. She was tall for her age, standing at about five feet eight inches. That was extremely tall for a third-grader. Her gray eyes were captivating, and he seemed to fall into a spell whenever he was in her presence. He had been trying to stay away from her but couldn't. It was like she was a magnet. Whenever he was with Precious, he thought about Beautiful. His guilty conscience beat him up occasionally, but it wasn't doing enough to make him stop doing what he was doing to these two children.

"I'm finished now. I was going to use the restroom and then get back in bed with Precious." Beautiful stuttered with fear, and tears caught in her throat.

"Don't rush; come sit over here with me." Big Man pulled a chair from the kitchen table, sat down, and patted his lap. Tears rolled down the young girl's face, but he ignored them. All he saw was her indescribable beauty.

Beautiful's feet felt like cement blocks; she couldn't move one inch. She was scared. Her mind was telling her to run for her life, but her body wouldn't respond. Every time she was in his presence, a feeling would come over her. It often made her want to throw up. The hair on the back of her neck stood up, and when she looked down at her arms, she had chill bumps. She didn't know what he did to Precious, but she knew what he did to her, which wasn't right. No man should do that to a child, but she didn't have anyone to tell.

He motioned for her to sit on his lap again, and the conversation that she had earlier on the playground with Precious played in her head.

"Big Man gives me anything I want. That is how I got my Casio keyboard, Nintendo, and video camera. I have got all the name-brand clothes now. My momma wasn't buying me the good stuff. At first, it used to be so bad, but I know that is how he showed his love for me. He is like my daddy and my boyfriend. I ain't never had a daddy, so I do everything he tell me to do because I don't want him to leave me and my momma. I'm eleven years old, I ain't never had a daddy, and my momma ain't never had a man. He is good to us." Precious sucked her thumb as Beautiful looked at her with her eyes bucked. She couldn't believe he'd made her think it was all right.

"But what he is doing to us is not right! He is supposed to do that with your momma. She is his woman; she is a grown lady. We are just little girls." Beautiful said, feeling sorry for her play cousin.

"Do I look like a little girl?" Precious said, standing up.

As she stood up, Beautiful looked at her. It seemed like overnight, Precious' body had changed into that of a grown woman. Her breasts were huge, and her hips and butt poked out so far that no clothes could hide her shapely figure. Coupled with her height, Precious looked twice her age.

Beautiful sniffled as she stood frozen in place. Her mind raced, wondering how to escape without waking Aunt Beth and Precious.

"You like those new Air Jordans that I bought Precious yesterday? If you sit on my lap and let me whisper in your ear, I will have a pair for you when I come home from work in the afternoon." He tried to adjust the erection that had started to form in his shorts, but he couldn't. He just opened his legs more to make himself comfortable.

She could feel the bile start to rise as her eyes fell on his crotch. He didn't have on any underwear. His hairy balls were visible, and his private was poking out of his shorts. Beautiful knew that she was going to be sick. She turned her head so she wouldn't have to look at him, and as soon as she did, the vomit shot out of her mouth like in the movie *The Exorcist*. She couldn't hold it back any longer. Between the thoughts of what he had done to her the last time and watching him staring at her like a gargoyle with a dry Jheri curl and those big eyes poking out of his skull, she was sick to her stomach. The entire contents of her stomach now stained the dingy white kitchen tile. Red liquid sprinkled with chunks of food covered the floor.

"You must have drunk too much juice. Clean this mess off the floor, and I will help you clean yourself up." Big Man got up from the table, took a fresh roll of paper towels from the top shelf and handed it to her. He rubbed a tear from her cheek. "Don't worry, I know how to make you feel better."

Beautiful used nearly a roll of paper towels to clean up her mess. She wanted to wash her face and hands and brush her teeth so badly. She felt so gross. As she threw the last remnants into the gray metal trashcan by the back door, Big Man walked back into the kitchen. Beautiful started to make a run for it.

He clamped his hand on top of hers on the doorknob; the dirt from his job digging graves was still under his fingernails. "I thought you were staying the night."

"I changed my mind. I just want to go home and get cleaned up. I need to rest because it will be time to wake up for school soon." Beautiful's voice trembled as if she was standing outside in the cool air.

She didn't want him to touch her. She promised herself that she would never come back to Aunt Beth's house when he was home again. Beautiful felt sorry for Precious. She didn't understand how she could program herself to think that what Big Man was doing was right. She didn't want him to think he could buy her stuff, even though she needed it, and keep doing what he was doing.

He pushed her against the door and pressed his heavy body onto hers. His breath was coming fast as his hands groped her through her clothes. His breath smelled just like the Big Red gum he chewed constantly. Beautiful wasn't developed yet like Precious, but his hands roamed her body as if she were. Chill bumps sprang up as her flesh crawled with his every caress.

"No, please don't do this to me. I am just a little girl. If you let me go home right now, I promise I will never come back over here, and I won't tell a soul what you are doing to Precious and me. I promise!" Beautiful pleaded with him repeatedly as tears soaked her face.

Big Man turned and looked over his shoulder to ensure no one was coming. He then scooped her up in his muscular arms and carried her a few short steps to the living room. After dumping her on the sofa, he immediately reached for her sleep shorts. Wrestling with her wasn't on his agenda, but he knew it would be accessible after the first time, just like it was with Precious.

Beautiful held onto her shorts so tightly that her knuckles were turning white. Her body shivered with fear because she knew no one would help her. She was defenseless against this grown man. He had kissed her, touched her private areas, and made her touch his before, but he had never stuck his thing in her.

He did it to Precious, and she said it hurt her badly. She continued to sob silently and thought about how there was supposed to be a God and angels in heaven. It couldn't be if this were happening to her. He pried her legs apart and laid on top of her. She was still holding onto her shorts. He had given up on trying to pull them down. Instead, he had torn them a little in the seat and was now forcing himself between her legs. He clamped his hand tightly over her mouth as he thrust himself inside her.

Beautiful wanted to ball up in a knot; the pain that shot through the lower part of her body felt like fire. She wanted to die as he moved back and forth on top of her, breathing hard in her ear.

Chapter One

THERE IS NO PLACE LIKE HOME

Coach K had been calling Honesty's phone since he woke up that morning from one of those dreams he'd have now and then about Beloved. The dream reminded him of how much she was like her mother. She was Beloved's carbon copy, with her model looks and how she acted. He needed to go to the hospital to check on Killa, but he wanted to spend time with his oldest daughter today because it always made him feel close to his only true love. He couldn't tell if the dream had happened before and he was reliving it or if it was just a dream. He was sure that he would figure it out. It made him happy and sad at the same time. It had been years since Beloved had come to him in a dream.

Coach K put his cell phone down, rolled out of his king-size bed, and decided to get ready to start his day. He promised himself to stop at the gas station and play all the numbers associated with Beloved. Maybe he would hit.

Deciding to drive to Alpharetta for a good night's sleep was probably not a good idea. He could barely sleep with so many things on his mind. When he closed his eyes, all he could think about was what he had planned for Beautiful.

Being in the mansion alone made him realize how lonely he was. Thoughts of Jazmeir crept into his mind as he took off his tank top and looked at himself in the mirror. Coach K had to admit that he still looked good for his age. He only had two gray hairs in his full beard, his caramel skin was flawless and youthful, and his eyes still shined like when he was twenty-one. The muscles in his arms were bulging, just like the ones on his chest, and even though he didn't go to his in-home gym as much as he used to, he remained in shape.

Jazmeir probably didn't even look at him like that. He knew that he shouldn't be looking at her like that. She had a son by his mentor, Black Sillk, and she used to be Slow Poke's lady. But be that as it may, she was beautiful, intelligent, fine as wine, single, and had been on his mind since he met her.

Coach K's phone started to ring. He looked around for it and remembered leaving it in his bed. He dived on the bed and answered it on the last ring.

"Uncle K, I'm here. Can you or one of the kids pick me up from the airport?" a young man's voice said from the other end.

He knew it was coming soon, but he had been dreading the moment. Lil' Pokey had come home from college on the West Coast to bury his dad. He had been so caught up in everything else going on that he didn't remember until he heard Lil' Pokey's voice that he hadn't even told him about Killa and the tragic car accident. They were thick as thieves growing up; the news would devastate him.

Coach K had always looked out for Lil' Pokey. They had a special connection. He didn't want his father's wild ways to get the best of him, and that was one reason why he had suggested that Lil' Pokey go to the West Coast for college. Paying for his full ride to USC wasn't a big deal if it would save him from the streets.

Lil' Pokey was different from Killa; taking a man's life gave him a high. He was cold-blooded, and he went looking for trouble. Coach K remembered being like that before he had kids. The trouble always found him because it seemed like he was right there to pick up the phone whenever it called. His juvenile record was as long as Bankhead Highway with Veterans Memorial included. Coach K knew that sending him away would be the only thing that would save his life. Lucky for him, Lil' Pokey had the grades, and all he needed was the money and a few handshakes to make it happen.

Before he turned fifteen years old, Lil' Pokey had killed three men. Coach K and Poke had covered up the murders. The last body they had to clean up was on his spring break vacation to Miami during his senior year in high school. He was a beast; he hunted down his prey and killed them before they knew what was coming. Coach K admired his skill because he was a killer, but he was scared of him at the same time. Lil' Pokey was only a child, and he had done things that men twice his age had yet to do. Coach K would never forget the look he had in his eyes when they found him in that hotel in Miami. He was holding a man's beating heart in his hand.

Coach K stared at the phone, and then he responded. "So much is going on right now, Lil' Pokey. Take a car service to the address I'm about to text you. It's money there to pay them. I will see you when I come into the city." Coach K rubbed his hand over his beard and peered closer in the mirror. He thought that before this was over, his beard would be filled with gray hairs.

He finished undressing and entered his walk-in shower. As the scalding hot water ran over his body, he thought about everything happening. His best friend had turned into a snake and had to be eliminated. His son had lost a leg, his girlfriend had died, his daughter had been robbed and nearly blown up, Concrete was lying in the hospital in a coma, and Loyalty was pregnant. The past few months had been hell. He couldn't believe that he only had two gray hairs. But then again, his head was shaved, so there is no telling what would be growing up top.

———————

Lil' Pokey grabbed his MCM duffle bag off the carousel as he slipped his phone back into his pocket. He had been calling Killa's phone all morning. He knew his cousin would be excited to come and scoop him up. But then again, he knew from their last conversation that Killa had fallen in love and was spending more time with his girl and her son. But damn, it still was strange that he didn't even reach out and call him to check on him, nor was he the one to break the news to him about his dad. Lil' Pokey would just have to take that up with him when he saw him. Between being all in love and working for Gigi, he knew there had to be a few seconds in the day when Killa could have just picked up the phone.

He walked outside the terminal and looked around. All he saw were town cars and shuttle buses. "Fuck it, I will just catch the MARTA train into the city. I haven't done that in years." Lil' Pokey adjusted his book bag on his shoulders and headed toward the Marta station. His tall frame was identical to that of a professional basketball player. He had never seen his mother, but his father always said she was tall.

Sports had never been his thing, even though basketballs were shoved into his palms throughout his childhood. He preferred the feeling of a gun or a book to a ball any day. He couldn't help it. Uncle K made him promise that he would put the guns down, and he did, but that didn't stop him from finding other ways to handle his business. Lil' Pokey had grown wise in his years away from everyone. He was focused on his studies, but he couldn't help the feeling that he got when he held someone's life in his hands. The difference between then and now is that he was getting paid top dollar to do it, and he didn't need his uncle and his dad to clean up his mess. He was the master of the killing game on the West Coast.

Once inside the Marta station, memories flooded his mind of when he used to cut school and ride the trains all day, people-watching and listening to music. The transit police never bothered him because he appeared older due to his height, but when viewed close up, Lil' Pokey had the same baby face he had when he was twelve years old.

He remembered going home to an empty house and an empty refrigerator. He always knew where his dad left the money, so he ate out daily, except when he was with Uncle K. All the take-out and delivery restaurants within a ten-mile radius knew his voice and order by heart. He was an only child with no mother and a father who loved the streets more than he loved him. Thank God for Uncle K. He didn't know where he would be without him.

His phone vibrated as he stood, trying to figure out how to pay for his trip. He pulled it out and saw that Uncle K had texted him the address. Things sure had changed from the last time he had rode the MARTA. The days of the tokens and paying with cash were long gone. He had to get a Breeze card, and that task seemed difficult.

Minutes later, Lil' Pokey settled into a seat on the northbound train. His backpack and duffle bag occupied the seat next to him. He wanted to listen to music in his headphones but couldn't because he needed to be fully aware of his surroundings.

He gazed out the train window and saw that the city had changed so much in the two and a half years he had been gone. All the housing projects had been knocked down, and there was no money to replace them. He wondered to himself, *where did all the people go, where did the crime go, where did the junkies go, where did all my friends go?*

Uncle K had made him promise not to sneak into the city while he was away and to cut off all contact with everyone. He wanted him to have a fresh start, which he had on the West Coast. No one knew of the boy whose mother had abandoned him on his father's doorstep or who had spent the majority of his time by himself thinking of better ways to take the life of another.

On the West Coast, he was a kid who came from wealthy parents, was straight-laced, had no drugs or alcohol, and had no girlfriend because he was so into remaining at the top of his class. He was the best-dressed and most popular shy guy during the day on campus. At night, he was a killer for hire.

Chapter Two

A DREAM, A SIMPLE FANTASY

Loyalty tried to make her body relax in the uncomfortable recliner, but she knew that even if she were at home in her California King platform bed, she wouldn't be sleeping, much less relaxing. She kept looking down at her cell phone in her lap. She had not received a call from K.J., so she knew he was done with her. He didn't even give her a chance to explain herself. He was now acting as if she didn't exist. Although everything wasn't her fault, she should have contacted him when she got home. Especially after the fabricated stories about her were all over the blogs. She felt her world crumble around her, but she had brought this on herself. She rubbed her stomach and noticed a little pudge. Loyalty realized it could be much worse as she looked over at her brother.

She and Killa were damn near twins. They shared the same face; they were the same age but had different mothers. His eyes were closed, but his eyeballs were moving back and forth. He was probably having another nightmare. Her brother had lost the love of his life and a leg in a blink of an eye. There was no way possible that Killa would ever be the same.

She got up to go and get him some crushed ice and juice. She also needed to stretch her legs. Her father had asked her the night before if something was wrong because he could see it in her eyes. She told him no. One thing was sure: Coach K was so in tune with his children that they couldn't lie to him. He just wanted to hear the truth from her.

Instead of stopping at the nurse's station, Loyalty decided to go downstairs to the gift shop and grab some snacks, maybe find one of those car magazines her brother loves. The first thing she saw when she got into the magazine section was K.J. on the cover of the *NFL Insider* magazine. She tried to hold the tears back, but it was like the dam broke as they flowed down her face. Loyalty used the back of her hands to wipe them away, but they kept coming.

She grabbed a Cosmopolitan, a Source, and a Car and Bike magazine and headed toward the counter. She picked up three packs of salted almonds, a king-size Reese's Peanut Butter Cup for her brother, plain Lay's potato chips, a Coke, and a Starbucks bottled Frappuccino. As she reached into her wallet to pay, a man wearing electric blue scrubs and black Crocs reached behind her and laid a black American Express card on the counter.

"Your beautiful face with those crocodile tears can get the entire store. Are you sure that's all that you want?" His deep voice made the baby hairs on her neck stand up.

Loyalty had been crying so much lately that she didn't have any mascara. She was sure that she looked a mess. Her hospital attire had become a uniform: a trapeze shirt, leggings, and her favorite Tory Burch wedge Mary Jane shoes. Her hair was pinned up in a messy ponytail. She hadn't pulled a comb through it in a week. She was sure she looked like she felt, yet he said she was beautiful.

Loyalty inhaled slowly to pull herself together, and her senses were assaulted with Bond No. 9 cologne and Dial soap. Her hands immediately went to push back all the loose strings of hair around her face before she turned around. She was going to try her best not to sound like a bitch, but if the man wasn't her dad or her brother, they could go and jump in the Chattahoochee. She hated the male species right now.

When she pulled her Black card from her purse, the cashier took the card off the counter and prepared to charge Loyalty's purchases. "I can pay for my stuff, but I appreciate it though." Her voice dripped with venom.

The cashier took her Black card from her hand and put the man's Black card back on the counter. As she bent down to sign her receipt, she could feel his body heat and hot, minty, fresh breath on her because he hadn't moved one step. Loyalty grabbed the black plastic bag, put her credit card back into her purse, and didn't look up. With her head hung low, she walked around the man, who stood well over six feet tall, without glancing up.

He looked at her as she walked away. The sadness in her eyes was unmistakable. He felt a connection to her, a longing to get to know her. He would have time to do that. She was up and walking around, so she wasn't a patient. She was crying, so that meant that whomever she was here to see had to be severely injured, which meant that she would be here visiting often.

"Marcus, do you know who that is or who she is visiting? I have to meet her." He asked the cashier whom he stopped to talk to whenever they shared the same shift.

Marcus knew who she was, even though she wasn't dressed fancy or made up. It was Loyalty Rasheed, a well-known Atlanta socialite. She had been in all the blogs lately, but he knew who she was because her family was considered Westside Royalty. Her brother had lost his leg last week in a fatal pile-up on the highway, and he was shipped there early the morning before.

The chief of staff had notified them not to release any information on the Rasheed family to anyone. His heartbeat sped up because he didn't know if he should tell what he knew or let the doctor find out for himself. "Dr. Ryan, that's Loyalty."

Leigh walked into the room with the blue bottle of her favorite wine. Her hips swayed from side to side as the long hair flowed down her naked back. She had texted Killa and told him to call her before he was on the way home, but he didn't.

The keys rattled on the other side of the door as she put the bottle on the nightstand next to the wine glasses and the little dark red Cartier box. She lay on the bed, threw her head back, and parted her bright red lips. Waves of hair fanned out around her body, and she looked like she was posing for a centerfold shot. Killa had never seen her with long hair before. Her red and black La Perla underwear set fit her curves perfectly.

Leigh closed her eyes as she heard the love of her life's footsteps on the hardwood floor coming toward her. She knew it was time, now or never. She held her breath as she felt Killa put pressure on the bed as he sat down.

"Baby, you look better than all of Victoria's Secret's Angels, every video girl, and all the centerfolds, and you belong to me. What a way to greet your man. If I knew you had this planned, I would've come home hours ago." Killa's eyes roamed up and down her body as he kissed her red-stained lips. Not a stretch mark, scar or dimple anywhere.

He looked at her flawless face, which was beautiful, but her eyes held his attention. They were filled with nothing but love for him, and he knew it. The look in her eyes mirrored the feelings in his heart. This woman was going to be his wife. He didn't want to rush it but knew he had never felt this way about any woman in his twenty-two years. He couldn't wait to talk to his dad.

Leigh got up from the bed and walked around to the nightstand. She poured two glasses of wine. She downed one glass and poured another before handing Killa one. He wasn't a drinker but took the glass from her anyway. After all, what could one glass hurt?

She reached her glass toward his for them to toast. "To the three of us, now, always and forever." Leigh had fallen head over heels for a man who not only loved her but loved her son as well.

She took a sip and put her glass back on the nightstand, then picked up the red box beside the wine bottle and got down on one knee as the tears pooled in her eyes. "Killa Rasheed, Will you marry us?"

They say when you know, you know. Killa was in shock as he stared at her on her knees on the side of the bed. She had just met his dad a month ago, and his sisters had fallen in love with her and her son. They had a perfect fit as if they were meant to be. He was speechless; his heart was telling his mind to tell his mouth to say yes, but the words wouldn't come out. Time seemed to stand still as she looked him in his eyes, waiting for him to reply.

When he didn't, Leigh stood up and looked down at him sitting on the bed. She was in shock. She just knew that he was going to say yes. She wiped her tears, smearing her makeup, but she didn't care. She left the bedroom door, and her red-bottomed heels clicked on the hardwood floors until the sound faded.

Killa jumped up, screaming, " Leigh, yes, I will marry you. I love you. Leigh, Leigh! Please don't leave me! Leigh, please don't leave me!

Leigh, why aren't you answering me? Leigh turn around!" The hallway seemed even longer as she walked away and suddenly disappeared from his sight. He hollered out one last time at the top of his lungs. "Leigh, Please! Please don't leave me!"

Chapter Three

I WILL BE YOUR FATHER FIGURE

Beautiful looked at herself in the mirror of the private bathroom inside the office at *Gigi's Pleasure Chest*. So far, so good; no one knew the difference yet. She had avoided all the important people, and everyone else thought she was Gorgeous. She played the role like a champ because her life depended on it.

Gorgeous godfather Ponchees had called and scheduled a meeting between her, him, Coach K, and his girlfriend, Sam, for the next day. This meeting would make or break her because these people knew Gorgeous best. She had been telling them over the phone that she had people out looking for her sister and that she had been spending all her time with Concrete since Honesty was away on her trip. She needed more than the same face to keep up the charade. There had to be a way to postpone the meeting again.

The knock on the office door startled her. She glanced at herself and wiped her sweaty palms on her slacks. That is one thing that she and her sister didn't have in common. Ever since Beautiful could remember, she'd always had sweaty hands and feet.

As a child, her sneakers smelled worse than her brother's. In middle school, she remembers going to the doctor and being diagnosed with hyperhidrosis, which is the name for the abnormally excessive sweating that occurred no matter what.

The knocking turned to a banging as she rushed to it. She forcedly pulled the door open, ready to curse out whoever was on the other side. But she couldn't; she rushed forward into his strong arms. Her brother, Handsome, had returned home. Tears were about to start falling, but Beautiful couldn't let them. Gorgeous was always strong and never showed emotions.

She swallowed hard and tried to compose herself before she looked into his eyes, eyes that mirrored hers. The crystal-clear gray eyes were the only thing all three shared. She knew her sister must've contacted their brother and told him what was happening. She had only talked to him briefly, and she hadn't seen him since he was released from the hospital and allowed to continue his cancer treatments in Baltimore, where he played for the Ravens. She felt guilty because she knew her brother would have been with her every step if the shoe was on the other foot. Even though she was older than him, he was like her father. She had stayed away from him because she knew she was disappointing him.

Handsome had come back to a war between his two sisters, whom he loved to death. He didn't want to see either one of them hurt. Both girls were beasts in their own right, but he felt that Gigi would win the war, even if Bea won a few battles. It may seem like it on the outside, but they were not built the same, and he knew it. He had to stop this before any blood was shed. They're triplets; they were in the womb together for almost nine months and spent the first nine years together. Distance, money, or status couldn't erase that.

He let his sister go from his embrace and walked into her plush office. Handsome hadn't been in the club since he flew in for the grand opening. He was proud of Gigi's accomplishments. She had learned so much from being under Black Sillk all her life. The three of them had taken separate paths. They all were given a fair chance, although Beautiful seemed never to be able to find her way. She was so much like their mother, Solitaire. She always had been, just floating, going wherever the wind may take her.

Solitaire had died of AIDS after years of using crack and heroin, being institutionalized for schizophrenia, and being on the streets. That was not the way that he wanted his sister, Beautiful, to turn out, but it seemed like that was where she was headed if Gigi or whoever she had fucked over didn't kill her first.

Beautiful considered tomorrow's meeting a test, but this was her final exam. If no one else knew her, her brother, who was born a few minutes after she was, definitely did. She was on the easy street; if she could fool him, her entire plan would flow effortlessly.

She took a seat behind the desk and tried not to do anything that would signal who she was. "Can I get you anything from the bar or the kitchen? We have a five-star chef who has been with us for about a year. We are known for our delicious food." Beautiful tried to hide her nervousness.

"I never turn down a good meal, but we will get to that later. When I talked to you on the phone last week, you acted like you were at the end of your rope with Bea. What has happened since then? You are awfully calm now. Please don't tell me that you have found her and harmed her. That is still our sister, for Christ's sake." Panic filled Handsome's voice as he loosened his tie and made himself comfortable in the lounge chair.

He had flown in from New York. He met with Nike's marketing department because his first pair of sneakers was scheduled to drop next fall. Jet lag had him feeling down, but he knew not to show it because Gorgeous would be on him like she was his doctor. He had been cancer-free for the last year and a half, but she still worried about him like a mother hen.

Beautiful wanted to get up and run. She was becoming more nervous by the minute. Being alone with her brother was stressful. She was scared he would be able to read her like he used to when they were little. Sweat pooled under her arms, and she wanted to remove the cashmere sweater, but she couldn't because then Handsome would see her arm filled with tattoos. She needed something to cool her off and calm her down. To provide a distraction, she picked up the office phone and called downstairs for a server to come up and take their order.

"Things have been so hectic around here this afternoon. I need something to calm my nerves. I never realized how much Concrete kept things in order until now."

Chapter Four

CAN'T JUDGE HER

K.J. sat on the sofa in his den with his foot on the ottoman. This was his second injury in the last two weeks. His head was not in the game, and his heart was in Atlanta. First, he had a concussion during the scrimmage, and now he had sprained his ankle in practice. He couldn't think straight, and it all had to do with Loyalty. He felt as if a part of him was missing. He didn't want to admit this to himself, but he hadn't felt this bad since the day his father didn't make it to his first recreational football game, and he found out later that he had been murdered. His life changed dramatically that day, like when Loyalty got on that plane.

"Nigga get your ass up, you cannot keep on moping around here." Koier hit the ankle brace that the doctor had put on his foot. She hated seeing her friend like this. It was like his world had ended, and it had nothing to do with these injuries.

She had taken it upon herself to research Loyalty and her family. She could not find much information online but had to do something to ease K.J.'s mind. His broken heart was driving her crazy. Koier had hired a private detective that one of her sorority sisters had referred her to in Atlanta. He had promised her some information by the weekend. She needed something to help him move forward, whether the information was bad or good.

"I can't get up, look at my damn ankle. Now, please leave me alone. What do you want, anyway?" he asked her irritably as he turned the volume up on the television. He wasn't interested in what they were saying on Sports Center, but he wanted Koier to leave.

"I just stopped by to bring the contracts that were delivered to the office, and I wanted to make sure that you were okay. You haven't been answering the phone for the last three days. Everything is going to get better. You have to focus on what you know. You know nothing about love, the heart, or relationships, but you know football. Use this to fuel you on that field. You can't be all over the place on the field because one wrong hit can ruin your career.

"Okay, okay, I hear ya man! I'm gonna look at them later. Just leave them right here and make sure that you lock the door when you leave out." K.J. used his hand to fan her toward the door.

"Alright, I'm leaving, but you need to get your shit together and get it together quickly. You act like you have torn a ligament or broken a bone. You sprained your ankle. You are okay. Get off your ass! Get your barber over here. You look a damn mess!" Koier walked out the door, twisted the lock, and slammed it hard when she left.

K.J. pulled out his cell phone. He wanted to dial Loyalty's phone number so bad, but his pride wouldn't let him. He just wanted to hear her sweet voice. He decided against it again and to call his grandmother; she always could cheer him up. "Hey, Big Mama. What are you doing up there?"

"Nothing much baby, just came in from outside picking me some mustard greens to cook later. How is that head and that leg feeling?

Better yet, how is my baby's broken heart? You talk to your pretty lil' girlfriend yet?" His grandmother's voice was always so soothing to him.

"No, ma'am, I haven't. I've been considering visiting you for a week or two. You don't mind, do you?" Talking to his grandmother wasn't enough; he wanted to go to Atlanta to be with her. She always had the answers or could point him in the right direction.

"Baby, you don't have to ask, can you come home? You bought this big ol' house, and it's just me puttering around in it by myself since your sister went off to school. Come on home and keep Big Mama company. You can see that girlfriend of yours while you are here. One of y'all got to stop being so stubborn."

K.J. knew that person had to be him. He had a feeling that Loyalty hadn't missed a beat. Right now, he didn't care what anyone had to say because everybody has a past, and he knew that if he was going to be with her, he would have to put her past indiscretions behind them both and stop listening to the naysayers. He just hoped and prayed that Loyalty would forgive him for his reaction.

Chapter Five

MOLLY WORLD

Beautiful tossed and turned in the bed. She wanted to go to sleep, but she couldn't. She was too on edge. The events from the last few days replayed in her head whenever she closed her eyes. She knew now that people were out looking for her. They hadn't figured out that she had taken her sister's place.

Her first mind told her to go and get a zip of the syrup, but she had taken a Molly when she was at the club, and she knew she shouldn't mix the drugs. She needed something to help her cope after Handsome left.

She had gone downstairs, and some No Pressure guys were there. She only knew who they were because of the chains around their necks. Trying not to be rude, she sent a bottle to where they were, along with three of her best girls on the day shift. One of the guys approached her when he was going to the restroom.

"Preciate dat, boss lady. We will find your sister and bring her to you no matter what it takes." He walked off to the restroom, leaving Beautiful sitting paralyzed on the barstool.

Now she was fiending for something to make her feel normal. It was bad enough that she was on them, to begin with, but Beautiful had come to the realization long ago that the drugs were the only things that helped her escape from her harsh reality.

What had started as her hearing Jamal and her mom in her head had now turned into her seeing them, too. She guessed what they had been saying all these years about her was true. She was indeed her mother's daughter. Solitaire used to talk to her Aunt Brilliant all the time after she died.

Moans erupted from the monitor, and she looked over to her night-stand where her laptop was open, and the closed-circuit camera was focused on her sister's badly bruised face. Honesty was still asleep in the chair behind Gorgeous with tape on her mouth and rope around her hands and feet.

Beautiful felt terrible as she looked at her sister's identical face on her computer screen. Both of her eyes were black, her bottom lip was swollen, and dried blood was on the side of her mouth from where her lip had been split. She knew that if her sister had the use of her hands and feet, it would have been a no-win situation.

Gorgeous was a beast when it came to fighting. When they were growing up, she beat up all the kids on the hill whenever they bothered the three siblings. All it took was one word, and it was like unleashing the dragon. She would turn from the sweet girl everyone loved to a straight-up monster. She was unstoppable; the fight didn't end until Gorgeous was too tired to fight anymore.

Beautiful had hidden them in the old warehouse across the street from her loft. No one would have a clue that they were there. After all, no one knew where she lived except Poke, who was dead. The ware-house was for sale and had been boarded up for over a year. It still had running water, and someone had rigged up some illegal electricity.

Beautiful could look out from her balcony in her condo and see right into the empty, open space. She hoped none of the occupants in her building were paying attention to the empty building across the street.

She lay on her back, staring at the ceiling and thought about the power that she felt when she was beating her sister after she had kidnapped them.

Gorgeous had just stared at her; it seemed like she'd stared through her. She didn't grimace or shed a tear. She took the repeated punches to her face as if she was used to it. She acted as if the pain didn't faze her at all. The force of the punches echoed loudly in the empty ware-house. It sounded like she was watching a boxing match.

Honesty sat in the chair, looking pissed. She cursed and spat at Beautiful, who retaliated by punching her in the side of her head. The blow knocked her out, and then she taped her mouth closed.

No matter how hard Beautiful tried, Gorgeous always remained undefeated. Even as she sat there severely beaten, with her eyes barely open, it was like she was looking at the camera and mocking her. She could've sworn that she saw a smirk on her face.

You're better than her. You are just like me. Take advantage of this opportunity and show the world what you are made of. Makes me proud. You have to be everything that I could never be. You are Beautiful Diamond. Quit acting like a tarnished stone. Do not let anyone stand in your way. Hearing her mother's voice was all that Beautiful needed to prompt her to get out of bed. There was still work to be done.

She hated how Molly made her feel when coming down from the high. She had been high, horny, and unable to sleep, with a headache for almost two days. Her nerves were shot. She was paranoid times ten. She wanted to do a line of coke, but she had snorted so much last week when she first took her sister's place that the inside of her nose was raw. Gorgeous had an entire room filled with bricks of cocaine, pure and uncut. Beautiful, I had never seen anything like it. She didn't want to overindulge, but her constantly running, painful nose told her she had.

Beautiful had taken Molly because everybody talked about how it made them feel. She had done Ecstasy so much when it first came out because it helped make her feel sexy when she was stripping at the club. But the Molly was an entirely different story. She had opened the clear capsule, sprinkled the crystallized powder into her Ciroc and pineapple juice, and took the drink straight to the head. She was cool, calm, and collected at first, and then it seemed like she was on high alert; even the sound of her phone ringing gave her the shakes. Now, here it was, two days later, and she was just starting to recover. Her head was banging like a bass drum, and she was starving.

"Bitch, I know you are looking at us. You can't hide forever. Once they find that delivery guy, all hell will break loose. He worked for a business, stupid. You didn't think they would notice when one of the employees didn't come back after making a delivery. You need to let Honesty go. She doesn't have anything to do with this. Why are you hurting innocent people? This is just between you and me. You are weak and unfit for life. You are just like your sorry-ass momma. You are going to suffer and die by yourself 'cause you have fucked over everything good in your life. Look, we might share the same body, face, and eyes, but we don't share the same soul. Bitch you don't have a soul, so you might as well be dead. You are going to wish you were dead because I don't care what we share; I'm going to sit and watch you die. I'm going to make sure that you suffer. My face will be the last face you see before you take your last breath."

Beautiful wished she'd taped her sister's mouth shut before she left them. She hadn't thought about the deliveryman since she had put the bullet in his skull. He was in the wrong place at the wrong time, just another casualty of war. She hoped her guy had disposed of his body well. Angrily, she slammed the laptop closed and shook her head as she heard Jamal's voice. This was too much for her to deal with. She needed to get high again.

Don't listen to your sister. Keep with the plan. You better not let Honesty go. Coach K took me from you, and he must suffer for what he did. You are calling the shots now. Don't let Gorgeous tell you what to do. You finally got everyone exactly where you want them. The voice of her dead boyfriend seemed louder than her mother's.

She shook her head back and forth, wishing the voices would leave her alone. Her waist-length black hair looked like velvet, and she grabbed handfuls of it and closed her eyes. If she weren't crazy already, Jamal and her mother would make sure that she was before it was over.

Beautiful knew she had a lot to do. Looking at herself in the mirror, she barely recognized herself, except when she looked closely. She was now Gorgeous Diamond until you looked into her eyes. Although they were still the same gray, they no longer shined bright. Her eyes were dull; the last little bit of light left her the night she found Jamal's dead body.

The beating on her door startled her from her reverie. No one knew where she lived, not even the workers she had recruited. She didn't even risk receiving mail here. Her heart was pounding so loudly she could hear it in her ears. She started to ignore the door, but instead, she went back over to her bed and retrieved her gun from under her pillow before tiptoeing to the door butt-naked. Beautiful looked out the peephole and couldn't believe her eyes. She stood back from the door, blinked repeatedly, and then rubbed her eyes. She was in shock. *How in the hell did he find me?* She thought to herself. She was going to need a hit of coke to deal with all that she had going on.

Lil' Pokey had called his guy on the West Coast, he was the best in the business, and he had located Beautiful, but even he said that it was hard. He hadn't seen her since Jamal's funeral. Their last meeting put a bad taste in his mouth. He couldn't get past the look in her eyes when he hugged her goodbye. He told her that he was going away to college on the West Coast, and he didn't know when he was coming back.

His heart expected Beautiful to beg him to stay, especially since Jamal was no longer alive. They could finally stop hiding their relationship and be together. But she just kissed him on the cheek and said to him without any expression, "I wish you the best," before walking away.

The door was snatched open, and standing before him was Gorgeous, butt naked with a chrome gun in her hand. She was breathtaking. Her jet-black hair was messy and hanging long, covering her breasts from his sight. She turned around and threw the gun on the sofa and pulled him into the condo before kissing him. The kiss was so passionate; it had caught him off guard.

He was stunned until he pulled away and looked into her eyes. He realized that it was Beautiful with black hair. Her naked body was on his like a second skin as she ripped into him like an animal.

Chapter Six

THIS IS AS REAL AS IT GETS

Reality stepped into the elevator and heaved a deep sigh as she put her pistol back into her purse and sat her computer bag on the floor. This vendetta shit was taking a lot out of her, and as bad as she wanted to take a sip of lean, she wanted even worse to be totally through with it.

All of her waking moments were either spent searching for information on Beautiful, hustling, or fucking. She knew that if she didn't have D.J. with her to help her, she would be in horrible shape. He was indeed her refuge during the storm, and she closed her eyes and thanked Allah for sending him to her. The maintenance man, clearing his throat, interrupted her prayer.

"Hey, Lil' Mama, I don't mean to bother you. I need to chop it up with you for a second, but I must do it outside of work." Brian said, staring intently into the most beautiful eyes he had ever seen.

"I've seen you around, so I know you have seen me around, so you know I got a man. A big ol' black man with a lotta pistols, a lotta money, and a major complex. We don't want no problems, shawty." Reality said cockily to the maintenance man.

"Yeah, I have seen you with your dude. I'm not trying to start any problems. It looks like Buddy lost his last fight from the looks of his face, so I know he ain't taking no prisoners the next go-round. But this is about some business, lil' mama. I just look like this. Never judge a book by its cover. Cause if we did that, then I would think I'm talking to a stripper who is headed to the gym instead of one of the most brilliant computer hackers in the south, Reality." Brian liked her snazzy attitude. She was a real spitfire.

The shock registered on Reality's face as his last sentence played in her head at least fifteen times before she opened her mouth. "Who are you, and what do you want?" She pulled her pistol out of her purse just as quickly as she had put it away and eased the safety off.

"Calm down, lil' mama. It's on some business. You are already doing your thing, but if you are ready to turn it all the way up, you will meet me here tonight at 8:00 p.m." Brian took out a slip of paper and wrote a phone number and an address on an old receipt he found in his pocket.

Reality looked at the torn piece of paper, and it was the Starbucks across from Camp Creek Market Place. She decided that she had nothing to lose. Wherever she went, her pistol did too. There is only so much a stranger can do inside a coffeehouse with a police precinct across the street. "I will be there. Next time, tell whoever told you about me to tell you everything about me."

"What do you mean? Yeah, they left out the way you looked, but they got everything else, I think." Brian said confidently because he knew that his boy had told him everything about how official Reality was regarding the computer game.

"If they did, you wouldn't have been surprised by the pistol. See, being who I am, it comes with the territory." Reality said, looking at him smugly, wondering who he was and who had sent him.

"I guess; I mean, if you say so. Things up here might be different from how they are down bottom. Only the criminals walk around with big pistols. Not pretty girls who are computer geniuses." Brian looked at the pistol that was in her hand and wondered if she could even shoot it.

Reality looked at him as he looked from her face to the pistol in her hand. "Yeah, I'm pretty sure if every pretty computer genius you met was Coach K's daughter, then they would have a reason to carry a big pistol and be able to shoot a moving target with their eyes closed or kill with their bare hands."

A cold chill went all over Dade County Brian as he heard the name Coach K. Trained to go was an understatement where this man was concerned, and if this was his daughter, she was a more than formidable ally and an enemy. How could his people have missed out on giving him this enormous piece of information? He might need to rethink his plan. He would see me after the meeting tonight. "So, are you gonna meet up with me or what?" Brian was trying his best not to let her see him sweat. He put his hands in his pockets and rubbed them dry.

"Yeah, I will be there." Reality got off the elevator in the parking deck and headed to the hospital to show her dad the info about the wreck, but with a lot on her mind about the big maintenance man.

Two weeks Later

Reality had been up since before the sun. Her phone was ringing nonstop. It was Wednesday, and she had a lot of money to collect. Her workers had been blowing up her phone so much that she crawled out of bed and entered the living room so she wouldn't wake D.J.

So many things had changed since that day in the elevator. Brian had hired her to hack into the patient database of the second-largest

HMO in the country. Tax returns are his business, and she didn't want to have anything to do with them. He had just gotten out of prison, but he told her that he was addicted to making money. She knew precisely what that addiction was like. She had it herself. Once he told her how much money he could make in a week, her ears shot up like a dog.

Reality had been on go since then, researching ways to make more money and how to do it without getting caught. She had a one-up on Brian; she was a computer girl who liked money, and he was a guy with a computer who wanted money. Since it was income tax time, she had been going hard without sleep. All of her workers, which she had nick-named 'The Money Team,' had been getting it in from sun up till sundown. She only saw D.J. as much as she did because they lived under the same roof now. She felt terrible because she had not even been over to see her brother since he had been moved to the Shep-herd's Center.

Leigh's funeral was set for Saturday. Reality knew that her brother wouldn't be able to attend the service. Her father had already paid for it. He wanted to free up whatever insurance money there was so Leigh's mother could start a trust fund for her grandson. Reality decided, as she stretched and sat on the sofa, that she would go and spend the night with Killa and bring him a gift to brighten his mood. He was going through a tough time right now. It seemed like she was the only one who wasn't going through anything traumatic. Everything was absolutely lovely on her end. She was in love, had money flowing hand over fist, and steadily invested it. She was drug-free, and she was at peace. Shit seemed too good to be true. She wanted to keep thinking optimistically, but it appeared that something was bound to happen when everything was perfect.

D.J. rolled over, but Reality's spot was empty. Her work phone had been ringing nonstop all night long. Reality had over twenty-five workers who were at her beck and call. She didn't take any shit and her operation ran with efficiency. It was income tax season, and Reality had so much money coming in that it was ridiculous. It was like she was getting high off all the money because she no longer smoked weed or sipped lean. All she did was pick up money, count, and crunch numbers to make more money.

She had told him over the weekend that she wanted them to start looking for a house, and if they didn't find one, they needed to have one built. He had been thinking the same thing. Although he owned six houses that he rented out and one that he worked out of, it was time for them to buy a home. So much was happening in the city, and both had condos. He needed a yard for his dog and hopefully some kids, even though he was not rushing her. Reality had just turned twenty years old, so she was still young, but she had seen and accomplished things in her life that even middle-aged women had not done. Being Coach K's daughter has its privileges. She had learned from the master.

He had fallen head over heels for this girl who was anything but ordinary, and he knew he wanted to spend his entire life with her. He was ready to pop the question, but both had so much going on. To some, it might seem like he was rushing, but D.J. knew he wasn't. Like his uncle always said, *it don't take all day to do nothing*, and he knew that he wanted to marry Reality. He just needed to find the right time and way to propose to the woman of his dreams.

His phones started ringing simultaneously, and he already knew what it was about. He had the syrup game on lock in the city. Everyone who was selling Lean got it from him. Gorgeous had hooked him up with a supplier who sent him more bottles than he could sell at first, but now it seemed like everyone in the city was on Actavis, and he was indeed the man to get it from. He was running low, and he had not been able to contact his connect. So now, he was fielding phone calls from all his people who were out or running low, too. D.J. got out of bed and called Gigi to see if she had talked to her people.

Reality ended the phone call and walked down the hall as D.J.

exited the other bedroom. She loved the way he looked at her. It never failed. She always felt butterflies when they looked into each other's eyes. "Hey bae, I haven't slept, but my major work is complete for today. All I have to do now is pickups. I love my Wednesdays and hate them at the same time. I think I will get back in bed for a couple of hours. Would you like to join me?"

She walked over to him, wrapped her arm around his waist, and looked up in his eyes lustfully. Reality was a virgin the first time they were together, and now she couldn't get enough.

"Okay, babe, that's a plan. I just got to call Gigi and see what's up with her people because they haven't answered my calls. I need to work quickly, fast, and in a hurry. It's a lot of people who depend on me to eat."

D.J. reached down and rubbed Reality's butt in the Victoria's Secret boy shorts. His penis started to rise instantly, and he knew he had to hurry up with the phone call. He headed into the bathroom with his phone on his ear. He had dialed Gigi's number three times, and it went straight to voicemail. D.J. washed his face and brushed his teeth. He dialed the number one last time before leaving the bathroom.

Reality was lying on her side on the leather platform bed that she had studded herself like the Christian Louboutin shoes. She had taken off her tank top and boy shorts, and she was naked on the bed waiting for him. Butterflies fluttered in her stomach; she was so anxious. She tried to blame it on the fact that she was about to make love to D.J. or that it was a money-making Wednesday, and she was probably going to bring home close to $75,000 today after paying her workers and giving Brian his cut. She didn't know what it was, but something felt wrong.

Reality plastered a smile on her face when D.J. entered the room. They were thinking alike because he had taken off the underwear that he had just had on when she saw him in the hallway. His long thick, chocolate penis swung from side to side as he walked over to the bed.

Her mouth instantly watered. If someone had told her months ago that she would turn into Superhead, she would have called them a liar. Reality loved to give D.J. head. She reached out, grabbed his penis, and took it into her wet mouth. It was so thick that it filled up her tiny hands. She looked up at him, and he looked down at her. His eyes filled with ecstasy as he moved his hips back and forth, fucking her mouth while running his hands through her hair.

Before long, he would be on his tiptoes, begging her to stop. She took pride in how she brought him to his knees every time. As she completely devoured him, and his moans, coupled with the slurps emitting from her wet mouth, filled the room, Reality understood why women ran the world.

D.J. pushed her on her back and kissed her in her mouth. The essence of his juices mixed in with her saliva after she had sucked him dry. He moved slowly down her body, planting kisses everywhere. She was wetter than the Atlantic Ocean, and his limp penis was instantly standing back up at attention when he put his hand between her legs. He was ready to dive in and surf on the waves of bliss that only Reality held, but he had to pleasure her as she did him. Not because he felt it was his duty but because she tasted better than a red velvet cupcake from Cami Cakes.

Reality arched her back and pressed her body forward. Her breast was in his mouth, and her wetness was in his hand as she rocked and rolled herself to her first climax. He played her like a bass guitar. Her moans and the smacking sound of her wetness provided the rhythm section as she dripped all over his hands. She brought his hand to her mouth and licked all the moisture and stickiness from it as he reached his destination and parted her lips. He went to work on her magic button with his expert tongue.

Her hands instantly went to his head as she grabbed a handful of his locks and prepared for a ride to ecstasy. After only a few flicks of his tongue, he put his finger in her middle and sucked on her magic button as she screamed out every curse word known to humankind. Orgasm after orgasm swept over her non-stop, making her feel as if she was on cloud nine.

D.J. had his second wind, and he was ready. He knew she would take control if he let her regain her composure. He flipped her petite body over on her stomach and lifted her by her waist. As he prepared to mount her from behind, he couldn't help but stare at her perfect ass that looked like he had shaped it with clay himself. It was the biggest thing on her, and it fit her perfectly. He looked toward the ceiling and thanked the creator as he slid into her wetness from behind. The tightness of her walls always took him by surprise. He tried to think about anything but the tight, warm, wet flesh that was surrounding his member.

Reality bucked up and started to throw her ass back towards him. D.J. continued to focus on anything, including work, but the feeling, coupled with her beauty, made him succumb to the building wave, and he started to pump feverishly into her. One of his hands palmed her round ass while the other played with her clitoris. He felt her walls clamp down on him, and he knew that she was about to climax, and he was ready to join her. He pumped three more times and collapsed as all the strength he had in him went inside her. He kissed her on the back of her neck as he used his last bit of strength to roll off her petite frame.

Reality sat up and looked at him, and then she leaned in to kiss him. "You better start nutting on my ass, or we going to have a boatload of kids running around here."

"Would that be so bad, baby?" D.J. asked her, loving that she didn't see any scars when she looked at him. She didn't see him as a monster or deformed. He was just D.J., Damn Jaimes.

Chapter Seven

DOA

Loyalty left the gift shop and decided to stop at the chapel. Right now, she needed help from all the gods. Even though she was raised in an Islamic household, she just felt like she needed to be closer to the higher power, and this was as good as it got in the hospital. She put her cell phone on silent before slipping it into her handbag.

She had been calling Honesty for the last three days and had yet to talk to her. That wasn't really out of character for her sister. When she is overwhelmed, she tends to go into her shell. It wasn't unlike her to shut down. She couldn't go too far into it with Gigi around. But Gigi had to search for her sister, and her right-hand man, Concrete, was in the hospital. She was probably overwhelmed already, without having to worry about her sister. Loyalty knew Gigi would put her foot down regarding her big sister, so she was not worried. Honesty was in good hands.

Loyalty wished that she had some good hands to be in. She needed K.J. so much. Killa was usually her backbone, and she felt so alone with him being in the hospital. Her dad had so much other shit to be focused on; the last thing he needed to be preoccupied with was Loyalty's man problems.

The chapel was dark except for the candles on the small altar. Loyalty walked to the front and got on her knees like she had seen it done on television and in the movies.

"I need help. I don't know where to turn, and I'm heartbroken. All I want to do is be happy and my family be okay. Why is that so hard? I have never done anything so bad to be getting what I'm getting. I went into this thing with K.J. with good intentions. I didn't want his money or his status. I wanted him. I love him, I'm in love with him, so why did this happen? Why didn't he give me a fair chance? I guess he believed everything in the blogs." She remained silent with her eyes closed and sat still as if the answer would come from the heavens.

After a while, the tears started to flow uncontrollably again, and she got off her knees, wiped her face, and headed back to her brother's room. Her dad or one of her sisters had to be there by now. Loyalty wanted a break. She had been at the hospital from sun up to sun down. She needed to go home, bathe, and sleep for a while.

Loyalty would cry her heart out one last time, fall out if need be, and hopefully wake up tomorrow with a new frame of mind because she couldn't continue to walk around like a zombie. She had two more months before college graduation, and the world was ahead of her. Her mother did it with no money, no family, and three kids; she knew she could do it. She was going to beat this. After all, it could be a lot worse.

Loyalty took her time walking back to Killa's room after she got off the elevator. Her mind was all over the place, with questions circling like vultures over a carcass. *How would she remain focused when she went back to class next week? How would her family handle the fact that she was pregnant? Would K.J. ever come to his senses?*

Doctors and nurses rushed past her, pushing a crash cart. She silently prayed for whomever they would help and entered the ladies' room.

The face staring back at her in the mirror seemed so unfamiliar. Dark circles were under her eyes, her hair stood on her head, and her lips were chapped. She couldn't believe someone had just told her that she was beautiful.

Loyalty turned on the cold water and splashed some on her face. Drops of water moistened her hair, and she reached into her purse and pulled out a hairbrush to make her ponytail neater. She looked in the mirror again, silently reassuring herself that she would go to the hair salon this week, and then she walked out the door.

Chapter Eight

FRIENDS 'TIL THE END...

Since leaving home earlier, Coach K had been running around like a chicken with his head cut off, and it wasn't even noon. He had a meeting with Ponchees and Gigi, and then he had to stop by the hospital and check on Killa. He had also promised himself he would stop by Honesty's place because he still had not talked to her.

He pulled up to the funeral home to pay for Poke's funeral. Even though his best friend did him wrong in the end, he felt that it was still only right that he take care of his funeral service and burial. They had been friends for almost thirty good years before jealousy and drugs destroyed their relationship. He had texted Lil' Pokey and instructed him to meet him there. He never received a response; he just hoped that he had gotten the message.

He hadn't been on the east side in a long time, but since Mack on Hollywood Road had died, he only dealt with Raleigh Rucker regarding funerals. Coach K walked through the front door, and the cold arms of death wrapped around him. He never could get used to the feeling that washed over him when he walked into a funeral home. His good friend, Mack, owned McCray Brothers Funeral

Home on the Westside, and he'd spent a lot of time up there. It didn't look like a funeral home. It was more like a residence filled with luxury furniture and pool tables. He still knew that in the back of the building was where his friend cut open bodies and got them ready for burial.

He laughed while he sat outside of Raleigh Rucker's office as Mack's voice replayed in his head. "All the bodies that I have prepared because of your hands, you have the nerve to walk in here like you are scared of a dead body. Boy, it ain't the dead ones that can hurt you. It's the ones that walking around that can harm you." Mack was a real stand-up guy on the Westside.

"Hey there, boy, how in the hell have you been doing?" Rucker's booming voice reminded him of Mack's, maybe because they were best friends. He grabbed Coach K in a firm hug and ended it with a hand-shake. The years had been kind to Rucker. He still looked good, with only a few lines in his face and a small patch of gray hair at his temples.

"Is he messed up badly?" Coach K asked, curious about the condition that Poke was in.

The front door opened, and in walked Lil' Pokey with a very solemn look on his face. Coach K looked at him and he reminded him of someone, but it wasn't his father. He couldn't put his hand on it. He shook the thought, walked over, and hugged him tightly.

"Hey son, I just got here myself. You didn't respond to the message, so I didn't know if you had got it. I'm happy that you made it home safely." Coach K stayed close to Lil' Pokey as they walked down a narrow hallway, following Rucker toward where the bodies were held.

It seemed as if all the air had been sucked out of the room as they walked in. Lying on the steel table was a heap of unidentifiable burned flesh. The smell took their breath away.

Coach K tried to make it out of the room, but he couldn't do so before the contents of his stomach came out of his mouth.

Lil' Pokey just stood there and stared, non-affected. He didn't display any emotions. He just stared at the steel table where his father's burnt body lay unrecognizable. "Uncle K, are you sure this is him? I have been around town today and heard the rumors of how Pops was wilding out. Are you sure this isn't a hoax so that he could get the hell on?"

"I checked his identity using his dental records, son because his fingerprints weren't attainable," Rucker said, wondering who had done this to Poke.

Lil' Pokey walked around the table in silence, looking at the heap of burnt flesh from every angle. "Test it again. I don't believe this nigga is dead. Use our DNA," he said in a low growl and walked out of the room, leaving Rucker and Coach K staring behind him.

Rucker looked over at Coach K, still wiping saliva from his mouth after vomiting. "What should I do?"

"Run the test like he said. This is what he needs so that he can be at peace. Do it." Coach K said to Rucker as he looked back over at the body.

He shook his head, thinking of the last time he and Poke were together. They were sitting at a table at the Beautiful restaurant eating lunch.

He could see the larceny in Poke's eyes as he made snide remark after snide remark. But Coach K still loved him. He had been his right-hand man since the early days when he was robbing Peter to pay Paul. Poke wasn't the best nigga in the world, and he didn't have a lot of friends by himself. Most people who dealt with him did it because of Coach K. He knew how he was; he understood his good and bad sides. Poke was the person who looked after Killa when his mother overdosed on heroin. He was also the one who had almost killed Killa.

"Drugs don't change a person... It only magnifies the behaviors that are already inside of them." Rucker said to Coach K as he pulled the sheet back over Poke's burnt body. He knew his old friend was having a hard time dealing with the death of his best friend.

———————

Beautiful took a deep breath and walked into the hospital room. She had been dreading the visit to Concrete, but she had to keep up with the charade of being Gorgeous. This would be her first time going to see him, which was really out of the ordinary for Gorgeous. When he was hurt in college and was in a coma, she had stayed at Concrete's bedside the entire time.

The hospital smell and the cold chill put a sour look on her face. Her designer heels clicked against the stark white hospital floor, and she walked down the hall to his room. She would make it a short visit; she just needed to say she had visited him. Beautiful pushed the door open, expecting an empty room, but Handsome sat at Concrete's bedside. Her heart pounded. She wasn't prepared to see her brother and had been trying to avoid him while he was in town.

"You must have been busy, Gigi. You haven't been down to see Concrete since I've been back home." Handsome looked at his sister as she stood near the door, looking like a frightened little girl. Something didn't seem right with her. He just couldn't put his finger on it. Maybe she was acting like this because of Concrete.

"Yeah, I've been swamped. I'm having to deal with the club and the other business. Concrete is down, and Honesty is out of town, so everything is on me. I'm good, though; I was built for this." Beautiful moved closer to Concrete's bed, reached down, and grabbed his hand resting beside him. He looked so peaceful as if he were sleeping.

"The doctors have been looking for you. They said that you are in charge of his medical care. They might have some questions or concerns to discuss with you. You can't disappear when Concrete needs you the most. You know that you are all he has." It was hard for him to believe that his sister had been so wrapped up in herself that she wouldn't be right by Concrete's side, especially when he was injured saving her life.

Concrete felt the sweaty hand holding his and he heard the voices. It was Handsome and Beautiful. His mind raced as he wondered where Gorgeous was and why Beautiful was holding his hand. Then it clicked in his mind. Something was wrong with Gorgeous, and Beautiful was pretending to be her. Gorgeous used to tell him about when they were little, how she and Beautiful used to switch spots with each other and fool everyone. He wanted to get up badly, but his body wouldn't let him. He tried to scream, but he couldn't. A low growl was able to escape. He had to do something. *If Beautiful is right here, then where in the hell is Gorgeous?*

"Did you hear that? Concrete just made a noise. He is trying to wake up. You see, you bring out the best in him. Let me go and get the doctor." Handsome ran out of the hospital room, leaving Beautiful with Concrete.

She tried to pull her hand away, but Concrete gripped it tightly. His eyes opened, and he tried to say something again, but it came out as another growl.

The doctor walked back into the hospital room, followed by Handsome. Concrete was lying in the bed with his eyes open and holding Gorgeous' hand. The doctor took his stethoscope and started to listen to Concrete's heartbeat. He then began asking him a series of questions. Concrete couldn't verbally respond because of the tube down his throat, but he did nod. When the doctor was there, Concrete never let Beautiful's hand go. He squeezed even tighter. He knew this was not Gorgeous; he needed to talk to Coach K or Ponchees because he did not want to put Handsome in the middle. He grunted more and reached up to pull on the tube in his mouth.

The doctor stopped him.

Concrete knew that he would be able to talk once it was removed.

"I will send the nurse in to remove your tubing. I'm going to schedule you for another MRI and brain scan to see what type of progress you have made. The therapist will also be in to see about your movement. Can you feel this?" The doctor removed the covers and lightly touched Concrete's toes with his ink pen.

Concrete did not feel anything. He shook his head no, and tears flowed down his face. He looked over at Beautiful, but she showed no emotion. She didn't say a word. This confirmed his belief that it was not Gorgeous standing beside him. Gorgeous would have been asking questions, crying, and trying to bring in specialists. This bitch, Beautiful, didn't have a heart. He let go of her hand and stared straight ahead. Whatever was wrong, he needed to get better quickly because he had to save Gorgeous and, more than likely, Honesty too.

"Thank you so much, doctor. I appreciate all that you are doing. We are going to get him back to one hundred percent. He is my right-hand man and my best friend to the end," Beautiful said flirtatiously to the doctor as she patted Concrete on his shoulder.

She never saw the darts Concrete was shooting at her with his eyes, but Handsome did.

Chapter Nine

I'M LOOKING FOR HER TOO

Coach K had been calling Honesty, but she still had not answered her phone. It was obvious that no one else had heard from her. Leigh's funeral was later on that day, and Poke's was the next day. He pounded on the door for three minutes before using his master key to enter the loft. Gigi said she was supposedly out of town, but her whereabouts were unknown. He knew she had been going through some things lately, but for her to take off alone during a time like this was so unlike her. What hurt the most was that she had not called him to tell him she was leaving, nor had she checked in while she was gone.

He walked in, and a creepy feeling came over him. He felt a chill, but the loft had been closed, and it was stuffy and hot. Coach K turned the air on and pulled his pistol out of his waistband as he walked around. Nothing seemed out of place. He could tell Honesty had put everything back in order after the break-in. He walked into the bedroom, which looked totally different from the rest of the house. The bed was unmade, clothes were thrown around, a broken vase was on the floor, and the picture on the wall was crooked. Something wasn't right.

Coach K looked in her closet, and nothing seemed to be missing, including her Louis Vuitton Damier luggage set she had begged him for on her birthday two years ago. It is evident that Honesty was not gone on vacation. She loved this luggage set and took it with her even if she was going on a trip three hours away. Panic filled him because he knew deep in his bones that something was wrong with his oldest daughter. His next stop was to see Gorgeous. She had to know something.

He pulled out his cell phone to call Reality. "I'm over at your building. Your sister isn't on vacation because all her stuff is still here. Run her credit cards and get me all the activity in her bank accounts. I'm about to go and see Gigi. Something is not right, and I'm about to get to the bottom of this right now."

Reality turned around from her workstation set up in D.J.'s home office. She had both monitors on her Macs up, working on things for tomorrow. She needed her crew to finish all the pick-ups before the banks opened at nine a.m. "Bae, when was the last time you saw my sister and Gigi together?"

"I haven't seen Gigi at all. I have just been hollering at her over the phone. She has been so busy. I don't have to deal with her much since I got my own plug now, plus I know that she has been so bogged down with all the other shit going on with the family, the boss man being in town, and Concrete laid up in a coma. I let her do her, and when we link up, it will still be all love, as always. You know I have nothing but love for Gigi; she is like a sister to me. But I did call her the other day and didn't get an answer. Why, what's up?"

He got up from the sofa, where he was lying down with his laptop on his chest, doing some research on his new business venture. He walked up to Reality and started to massage her shoulders. She leaned her head back, and he bent down and kissed her forehead. "Why are you looking worried?"

"That was Pop's on the phone; he just called and told me to run Honesty's bank activity and credit cards to see where she is. He does not think she is on vacation. I know he is a little bit paranoid about everything he is going through, but I didn't like the sound of his voice. I need you to go and pay your play sister, Gigi, a visit and see what is going on. You know how to read people, so don't say anything about Honesty being missing. Just bring her up in conversation and see what reaction you get."

Reality and D.J. had been in their own little world, and she started to feel guilty because she had not been paying attention to anything lately that didn't have to do with money or D.J. She shut down both of her computers and went to put on some clothes. She was going to go and see her brother before the funeral.

D.J. came out of the closet dressed and looking immaculate. She thought to herself, *this guy is such a class act.*

"I will meet you at the funeral home. I'm heading over to the club." He walked with his keys in his hands, looking like the Ralph Lauren Purple Label had been tailored especially for him. D.J. didn't believe a grown man should walk around with his clothes slouching, and his clothes always fit him perfectly. The pants fit his bowed legs, and the big H from the Hermes belt and the spike red bottom Louboutin high-top shoes made a simple pair of slacks and cashmere button-down look like he was about to walk the catwalk at a fashion show.

Reality ran to the door before he walked out of it. She reached up and pulled him down for a kiss. She kissed him like she would never see him again. She did that every time they were leaving each other. Killa and Leigh's situation made her realize that you never know what the next moment will bring, so always act like you might never see that person again.

She pulled away from his embrace. "I love you more. See you in a minute. I will check on Killa before I go to the service."

D.J. had been a loner since he could remember. He never had any family and didn't have many friends. He had run into Gorgeous about ten years ago when she was looking for her mother in one of his traps, and they had linked up and been A-1 since. She didn't look at him like he was disgusting or disfigured; she didn't even grimace the first time that she saw his face. When she got into the dope game, he gave her a few pointers and always was a listening ear or springboard for whatever she had going on.

After narrowly escaping the Feds three years ago on a major trafficking charge, D.J. decided to change the game totally. He changed his way of life, including who he hung around, where he hustled, what he hustled, and his religion. One of the only things that stayed constant was Gorgeous. She was like his sister and his brother wrapped in one.

He pulled into the parking lot of Gigi's Pleasure Chest, which was empty except for two cars. He noticed a new convertible Rolls Royce Phantom parked right in front. He figured that it was Ponchees' car. Rafek opened the glass door for him, and D.J. walked into the empty club and headed toward the back to go upstairs to Gorgeous's office. Rafek walked up behind him closely, which made him feel unsettled.

He turned around abruptly to face him. "You don't have to walk up on me like that, partner. I know where I'm going," he told him through his perfectly straight clinched teeth.

Rafek stopped as he watched the man with the scarred face head to talk to his boss.

Beautiful sat behind the desk, deep in thought, leaning back in the chair. She had been on edge since she visited Concrete a few days ago. She avoided everyone close to Gorgeous because she didn't want to slip up and blow her cover. Lil' Poke had been blowing up her phone, and she hadn't answered. Beautiful had been flooded with so many emotions since she saw Lil' Poke. Memories of her and Jamal were haunting her already, and then Lil' Poke reappeared like he didn't leave her at one of the lowest points in her life.

The tap at the door startled her out of her thoughts, and she sat up fast. It was probably Handsome. He had called her about six or seven times this morning when she was at the Rolls Royce dealership. She didn't answer because she didn't want to have to explain her purchase to her brother. "Come in," she said, her voice filled with exasperation.

"Hey, sis, I woke up with you on my mind and just came to check on you. I didn't want you to think that I had abandoned you since Reality and I got together, plus I also wanted to run something by you."

D.J. walked into the office and stood in front of the desk. Usually, Gigi would run around the desk and give him a hug or something. Instead, she just sat there behind the desk, her pointed blood-red nails tapping on the keyboard of a PC.

"I'm good, D.J. Just trying to hold everything in the road. My brother is in town, so he has been looking out for me, but you know that I miss my right-hand man." Beautiful was ready for him to either sit his ass down or walk out because she hated when someone stood over her like that. He was standing there staring at her. She was trying to see what else she should say to him. She didn't know much about him, just that he and Gorgeous were close, he and Reality were a couple, and he had been calling Gorgeous and she hadn't been answering.

"What happened to your Mac?" D.J. eyed the HP computer on the glass desk. He knew that Gigi hated PCs. She had told him that she had been in love with Apple computers since high school. He also noticed the Rolls Royce keyfob lying next to the computer with a yellow tag with writing on it.

"Oh, it has a virus." Beautiful watched him as he watched her.

He sat down finally in the chair facing her.

If D.J. were a dog, his ears would stick up. He knew now that something wasn't right. He looked into her eyes and knew then that this was not Gorgeous. "I guess I will meet your brother at the funeral, huh? You are coming to Leigh's funeral, aren't you?"

His eyes bore a hole into her. It seemed like she didn't want to make eye contact, and when he leaned toward her over the desk, she grimaced. D.J. grabbed the key fob and looked at it. He rotated it in his hand and then he read the yellow tag. Diamond was written on it in marker.

D.J.'s face was so fucked up that Beautiful had a hard time looking at him, and when he leaned close to her, she felt as if she was about to throw up. She swallowed hard and tried not to look at him without causing suspicion. "I doubt if I go to the funeral. I mean, I didn't know her. Do you see the Phantom outside? I had to get something to take my mind off all this bullshit. You know my Range got fucked up in the explosion, so I just went and copped me that." Beautiful felt herself growing flushed as he sat there looking back and forth at her and the key in his hand.

D.J. put the key back down on the desk. "So you changed your mind about it? I remember you being so against it when I told you that I wanted to go and get it."

D.J. had chills as he remembered the conversation he and Gorgeous had about how flashy they would be. She was against them getting anything flashier than what they already had, and she didn't want to draw attention to anyone in the organization. He couldn't shake the feeling that had come over him. It was like he was panicking, and he wasn't sure why.

Beautiful could not stand to be scrutinized. "Yeah, you know I'm grown, it's my money and I'm entitled to change my mind. My truck blew up for God's sake. What was I supposed to do? Walk around?" She brought up her Google account on the laptop and went to her Google Voice. Her cell phone started to ring. "DJ, I need to take this call in private. This is Ponchees. I will see you at the funeral tomorrow." She got up from the desk, pressed the button on her phone and walked in the hallway.

D.J. got up from his seat; he didn't even need to ask her about Honesty. He needed to call Coach K as soon as he left.

As soon as he was out of sight, Beautiful inhaled and exhaled loudly as she leaned on the wall at the top of the steps. As if his face wasn't creepy enough, how he looked at her took her over the edge. D.J. looked at her like he was looking right through her, and if this were the case, he would know that she was not Gorgeous.

Beautiful went down the steps to the bar as her heart pounded. She needed a shot of something strong to calm her nerves. She wanted a hit of coke, but a couple of shots of Patron would have to do. The bartender came to where she stood and poured a shot of Patron.

"Leave the bottle!" she said, plopping down on the barstool.

The bartender came around and stood in front of Beautiful. She wrapped her arms around her neck and leaned in for a kiss. Beautiful pushed her away forcefully.

"Gigi, baby, what's wrong? No one is here; it's just you and me. Why have you been tripping lately? You would think that since

Honesty is gone out of town, I would be with you every day, but that hasn't happened yet. You haven't even been home in God knows when because I have been going by there. So, who are you fucking with now? Are you just going to throw me away like that? I settled on being number two but refuse to be number three." She was outraged. Tears poured down her face as the woman who she had started to fall in love with looked at her like her feelings didn't matter.

"I got too much other shit going on to be worrying about you throwing a hissy fit 'cause I ain't been licking on you lately. Miss me with the bullshit." Beautiful poured another shot as she thought about the fact that her sister had been having an affair with the bartender and Honesty didn't know it. She would use this later as ammunition.

"Fuck you, Gorgeous Diamond. Fuck you!" the bartender shouted before she stormed off in the direction of the ladies' room.

Rafek walked up from somewhere in the shadows. "The shit just hit the fan, huh?" he said as he sat on the stool next to Beautiful.

"Lucky for me, I got a big ass umbrella."

Beautiful poured another shot, downed it in one gulp, and returned to the office.

Chapter Ten

IT'S SO HARD TO SAY GOODBYE TO YESTERDAY

The wind whipped hard, and the clouds hung low as the processional cars drove slowly down Cascade Road and turned into Murray Brothers Funeral Home. The dark sky appeared ready to open and release some of the tears that were built up inside of everyone. Leigh's mother was a member of a Salem Bible Church, but in a rush to let her daughter's soul be at peace, she opted for a small funeral service inside the funeral home that had handled Leigh's cremation. They had a very small family, so she didn't expect the chapel to be filled.

The mood was solemn as raindrops started falling on the mourners as they exited their cars and walked toward the sanctuary. No one rushed to get out of the rain or worried about clothing and hair as they filed into the building two at a time. The smell inside the funeral home was a mixture of death, bleach, perfume, and flowers.

Mrs. Johnston had not expected such a big crowd as she walked into the sanctuary holding Kaydence's hand. He had been taking it especially hard, and he didn't understand. She squeezed his hand reassuringly as she looked down at his tear-stained face. She felt so bad for him because she knew if he could say curse words to her, he would. He was so mad on the inside, and he was displaying it. He wouldn't eat, and he was barely sleeping. When she had gone into his bedroom two nights earlier, he was sitting in the middle of his bed with a picture frame in his hands, talking to it. When she heard what he said, she was about to tuck him in and turn his lights off.

"Granny is always talking about God and how he controls every-thing. Well, I hate God; he took you from me, he took my daddy from me, and now Killa is sick, and he might die. God is mean to me. I need you, Mommy, please come back. I don't need you to be my angel. I need you to be my mommy." Kaydence kissed the picture, laid it on the pillow beside him on his full-size bed, and got under his covers.

She stood in the door with tears steadily pouring down her face. She was mad at God, too; she knew that no matter how hard she prayed for understanding, she might never get it. It broke her heart into a million pieces again as she heard her grandson battle with what had happened to his mother. He was too young to have to go through this.

Toe-Toe, Nard, D.J. and Coach K huddled in the sanctuary lobby, deep in a conversation. People walked past them as they went in and took their seats. Things were not adding up, and they were trying to get to the bottom of it. All of them had the same suspicions.

"Man, it's some ain't right. I just came from seeing Gigi at the club, and that ain't the Gigi that I know." D.J. said, his words coming out a little louder than he wanted them to, but he had to speak on what was bothering him so much.

"I told Coach K that same thing a few seconds before you walked up. I went to the club over the weekend, and she looked like she was high, and I know what high looks like. Now shit, Sis just started drink-ing, and you know how she feels about us doing anything besides weed.

She hates drugs. She is getting on Nard about being on the Mollies so much." Toe-Toe chimed in.

"Aye, Coach, does Honesty say Gigi has been acting differently? 'Cause I haven't seen her. Whenever I go by the club, she isn't there. She hasn't called me, and she hasn't stopped by. Gigi usually stops by the spot at least once a week. She will chill with us and shoot the shit. Gigi will even join the crap game. She is like a ghost. You don't see her, but know she is in the shadows." Nard rubbed the stubble on his chin as he tried to figure out what was happening.

"Well, that's my biggest problem right there. I have not talked to my daughter since she went home from the hospital after the explosion. In our last conversation, she was saying that after the funerals and Killa was released from the hospital, she was going to go missing for a few days. Go somewhere with a beach and some sand. I assumed she and Gigi were going, but then I learned from Handsome that Gigi was still in town. That sent up a red flag 'cause I know that Honesty wouldn't just go nowhere by herself. I went to her place, and all of her luggage was still there, and it appeared that none of her clothes were missing." Coach ran his hand over his bald head nervously as he thought about the fact that his daughter might be somewhere hurt.

"Wait a minute, Handsome is in town? Dat nigga ain't even called me!" Nard wondered why one of his childhood best friends had not called to let him know he was back in his hometown.

"He called and told me he needed to talk to me about something important, but we never set up a time and place." Coach K said to Nard to soothe him when he saw the hurt look in his eyes.

"Y'all know Gigi is like my sister. She was the only person in the world loyal to me and there for me before Reality came along. I walked into her office and she looked at me like a stranger. Ever since I first met Gigi, she has always greeted me with a hug. This person sat at her desk and didn't get up. She never made eye contact and acted like looking at me in the face was bothering her. Since day one, we have formed a bond, and she has looked past my wounds. She could actually see who I am without these scars. Not this person."

D.J. had left the club thinking one thing, and now, after hearing what all the other guys were saying, he knew it was true.

"I have a powerful feeling about this, and only three people in the world can confirm it. One is missing, one is in a coma and the other one is Handsome." Coach K raised his voice louder than he wanted to as he walked out the funeral home's front door with D.J., Nard and Toe-Toe following him. The pit in his stomach had doubled in size as he feared the worst for his daughter.

———————

Leigh's body had been cremated, and her ashes were placed in two separate solid gold urns with diamond and emerald-encrusted tops. They sat on top of a mahogany table at the front of the sanctuary with three large poster-size pictures of Leigh. One picture was of Leigh as a child, the other was of her holding Kaydence when he was first born, and the last was of her, Killa and Kaydence, which had been taken a week before the car accident.

Many of her friends from school over the years had shown up, including church members and people from Bankhead Court. The sanctuary was standing room only. Leigh's mother did not realize how many lives her daughter had touched. As she and Kaydence sat in the front row, she realized that maybe she should have had the services at the church. Beautiful flowers took up the front of the sanctuary, and the fragrance filled the place. The jumbo projection screen played a slideshow of pictures of Leigh from birth to her death as soft, soothing music played. One of her elementary school teachers who mentored her and was also a pastor was officiating the service and doing the eulogy.

Reality and Loyalty sat in the pew side-by-side, holding hands. No words were spoken, but they had missed each other immensely. When they saw each other on the way in, they hugged and held on for dear life. Reality could see that her sister looked different. She had dark circles around her eyes and looked like she had lost weight. But most of all, she noticed her sister's growing belly. Loyalty was lean, with no stomach. She even had abs, whereas Reality just had a flat stomach. There was a question in her eyes as she looked at her sister, but she decided to wait to tell her what was happening instead of intruding. Reality knew that her sister was taking her breakup with K.J. hard, but now she could see why she had been isolating herself and spending all her time with Killa at the hospital. She was hiding.

Despite them being at the funeral for Killa's girlfriend, Reality's happiness could not be hidden from her sister. It was evident in her eyes, her stride and her smile. It was like love exuded from her pores. Loyalty was happy for her sister but was in a dark place. She was in a rut and needed to get out of it. She had sat at the hospital day in and day out and purged herself of all that she was going through to her brother as he lay in a coma. But now, that was no longer possible since everything had happened.

They directed their eyes to the front as Leigh was eulogized. Reality never let go of her sister's hand throughout the entire service, and now and then, she rubbed her hand or gave it a reassuring squeeze. The slideshow pictures highlighted that Leigh was a beautiful girl, and everyone had so many great things to say about her. As the service ended, Leigh's mother took the podium. She held her head high as she cleared her throat.

"Thank you all for coming. I didn't expect this turnout for my baby, so I chose to have it here instead of the church. Leigh was my only child and the rock of my heart. She was my heartbeat, my angel. Leigh was mature before she needed to be, but she wasn't grown. She stayed in a child's place and raised herself and me. She motivated me to be the person I needed to be; she was my light in the deepest hell. My daughter had perfect attendance from kindergarten until the day she died. She never missed a day out of school. Many nights, I wasn't at home to tuck her in or there to wake her up, but she still made it to school and made the best grades.

"I was out on the streets doing whatever it took for me to get the next high, and when I did come home and crash after a binge, it was my daughter who cleaned me up and fed me. My daughter never told a soul what was happening in her household, so the authorities never got involved. It was my daughter who nursed me back to health after she found me in a crack house, beaten beyond recognition and raped from asshole to appetite. So, if you are wondering why I can stand here before you and seem composed, it's because I always knew my daughter was an angel from heaven. So now, she is just back on high in her rightful place, next to the heavenly father.

"I'm hurt, yes. But I'm at peace because my daughter ensured I was well enough in body and mind to take care of her son. She raised herself and me, and now I can finally be a mother and raise him. My daughter always made sacrifices for me as a mother would do for their child. She worked a job, made clothes, and sold them to boutiques to hold the household down while I did a double course load in college to get my degree in social work. So, for all the hearts that are here and heavy for my loss, please know that I'm going to be alright. Keep Kaydence and Killa in your prayers because they need it the most. Again, thank you all for coming to her home-going services. I love you very much." She stepped away, and a few tears fell from her eyes.

A sudden high-pitched scream radiated off the sanctuary walls as Kaydence shouted, "No, Mommy, no. Please come down from heaven. I need you here." He got up and ran full speed out the door.

It seemed like every eye that had been dry throughout the service was now filled with tears as they watched the little boy in so much pain from the loss of his mother.

Chapter Eleven

YA BETTER BELIEVE IT...

They sat tied up in the chairs, with their backs to one another. Gigi had been trying to untie the rope that was cutting through her wrist. Honesty was irritable, hungry and in and out of consciousness. It appeared that when Beautiful hit her in the head with the pistol, she might have given her a concussion. The girls' legs were taped to the legs of the chair and Gigi had pains in her knees from being unable to stretch her long legs. No one had been in to feed them or allow them to use the bathroom. Gigi's stomach hurt from the hunger pains that were ripping through her, but she continued to work her long fingers on the rope to get them free.

The door slid open and Beautiful stepped into the warehouse in a pair of six-inch nude patent leather Louboutins, a red sheath dress, and a leopard print sweater. Her hair was piled on her head in a messy bun. She held a tray of drinks and carried two Zaxby bags in her other hand. She had not been to the warehouse in almost two days, and the smell of urine drifted throughout the dank warehouse. She walked over, put the food and drinks on the floor, and pulled her pistol out of her purse.

"Okay, I'm going to untie one of you. I will walk you to the restroom and back. You will eat and then feed the other. I will tie you back up and then I will untie the other and allow them to go the restroom. Anybody got a problem with that?" Beautiful looked at Honesty, who looked asleep with her head hung low to one side. The knot on her head had tripled in size, and there was a cut across the top of her eye from where she had been hit with the pistol. Beautiful then looked at her sister, who was staring at her with the same eyes; the only difference was behind her sister's eyes; Beautiful saw flames.

"Where ya lil' flunkies at, Dumb and Dumber? Untie me, you got me sitting in here soaking in my piss. Honesty has been in and out of consciousness ever since you hit her in the head with that fucking pistol. I need to check her vital signs to make sure she is all right." Gigi said to her sister as calmly as possible between clenched teeth.

Beautiful moved closer to where they were sitting, and Honesty appeared alive; her chest rose up and down with her breathing. "This bitch is all right, but it is kind of you to be worried about this pussy sucking hoe." Beautiful slapped Honesty across the face abruptly. "Bitch get up so you can apologize to me for spitting in my face." Beautiful said as she held the pistol like she was about to hit Honesty again.

"You hit her again, and I swear I'm gonna cut you up with a straight razor and pour salt into each and every small little wound that I plan on inflicting upon your miserable body. Trust and believe, I'm gonna definitely kill you. I'm gonna try to make that shit last forever, and the only thing that could stop me was if you were to put a bullet in me right now." Gigi's face turned bright red as she sat in the chair, staring at her sister. Her bladder couldn't take it anymore and the urine started to flow freely from her as she peed on herself again.

"I'm in control now, big sister. I got the crown and the key to the city. Calm down. There is nothing that you can do." The smile spread across Beautiful's face as the reality set in of how much money and power she possessed was menacing and evil.

"You still ain't shit, you around here doing what you used to do when we were little. Pretending to be me because I am who you have always aspired to be. That should make you feel like shit. I'm the one you look up to and only older than you by a few minutes. Your little pea brain couldn't come up with anything better to be than your identical twin sister when you grew up. We look alike, but we damn sure are not built alike. You are just like that sorry ass hoe that gave birth to you. Bitch you ain't good for nothing but some dope up your nose and some dick in your ass. You might have control but don't have it because you aren't being yourself, Beautiful. Bitch you got it by being me." Gigi glared at her sister with her eyes slanted. She wanted to kill her with her bare hands.

Honesty moaned in pain as she woke up. Her arms were hurting and tired from being tied behind her back. Her knees hurt from sitting in the same position for so long, and her stomach hurt because she was so hungry. She heard Beautiful and Gigi arguing. She could feel the venom spewing from Gigi's mouth. She had never heard her that mad before.

"Babe, you all right?" Gigi wanted to make sure that Honesty was okay. Beautiful had hit her hard with the pistol and her going in and out of consciousness had her worried.

"My head hurts like hell, my knees feel like I got arthritis, and my stomach is touching my back. Don't worry about me. We are going to be okay. The devil might put up a battle, but he never wins the war." Honesty couldn't see the food, but she could smell it, and her stomach growled as the aroma of urine and fried chicken filled the warehouse.

"You got some nerve calling me the damn devil, all the niggas in the city your daddy done killed or had killed. Now that muthafucker is the devil." Beautiful walked around and faced Honesty.

"Girl, you don't know anything about my daddy. My daddy is the reason a lot of niggas in the city are making money. Shit, he is the reason a lot of niggas still breathing. Hell you talking about? Get the fuck on with all the bullshit." Honesty couldn't stand anyone saying one cross thing about her mother or father.

"Oh yeah, I forgot. Dat nigga ain't yo' real daddy. He just rescued your ass so you wouldn't be an orphan." Beautiful had stooped low and was face to face with Honesty. She looked at the humongous knot on her head and the deep cut over her eye. If prompted, she would put one on the other side. She hated this bitch and everything that she stood for, partly because she was Coach K's daughter but mostly because she was closer to her sister than she had ever been.

"Bitch, you're just mad 'cause no one rescued your orphan ass. Didn't nobody want your ass then, and don't nobody want your ass now. You holding us here is only making more muthafuckers not like your ass, and you're not going to be able to escape their wrath. The only one you got in your corner is Handsome, and even he is not going to be able to keep the big dogs off your ass." Gigi knew as soon as she let those words escape her mouth that she had hit below the belt with her sister.

Beautiful strolled around to look at Gigi, still defiant and confident, sitting tied up, beat up, starving, and pissy. Her will was amazing; she was in awe of her. She wanted to be this strong. But like Gigi said, they looked alike but were not built alike. She was tainted, and her weakness and fear had probably landed her in this boat to begin with. Her thoughts drifted off.

Beautiful had been too scared to tell anyone and she stopped fighting after he finally took her virginity. She felt like she had nothing else left to fight for. Her dignity and her innocence were lost forever. She would just lie still, cry and pray for it to be over as soon as possible. Gigi wouldn't have had that problem because she would never have repeatedly put herself in that position. Big Man molested Beautiful at his house. He never came over to their house, so Beautiful felt she was at fault for what had happened because she could've just stayed at home.

"Why are you looking me up and down? You need to be staring me in my eyes. I'm everything you could never be. You can put on every article of clothes I own, dye your hair, drive my vehicles and even sleep in my bed, and you still ain't shit." Gigi taunted her sister as she looked at her, mirroring her entire style.

Beautiful busted out laughing loudly as she walked over to her purse. She pulled out the keys to the Rolls Royce Phantom Drophead she had just purchased at the beginning of the week. She shook the key fob with the double R in her sister's face. "Guess what, sister, these are my clothes. I sleep in my own bed every night. Don't nobody want to go over to that gigantic funeral parlor that you call home, and as far as vehicles, well bitch I'm doing it bigger than you ever did it. Of course, With your money, But that is just a technicality." She sneered sarcastically.

Gigi lunged forward out of the chair as her sister got so close to her that she could smell her mint-flavored breath. Her legs were still taped to the chair, so she fell forward onto her sister. A gunshot rang out, echoing off the walls of the empty warehouse.

Honesty's loud, piercing scream followed, and then there was complete silence.

Chapter Twelve

THE SWITCH UP

Coach K, Toe-Toe, Nard, and D.J. all stood around Concrete's hospital bed as Ponchees sat in the chair beside it. It seemed like everyone had Concrete on their mind.

He sat up in the hospital bed. He had lost a lot of weight, but he looked healthy. His face was filled with almost as much hair as he had on his head. His usually manicured fingernails were bitten down almost to the cuticles. But he was so happy to see that he hadn't been forgotten and that he didn't care how he looked. He hadn't looked in a mirror in what seemed like forever.

"I just walked in and sat down. That girl canceled another meeting with me, so I decided to come here to see if I could run into her. She has been to see Concrete once since he was hospitalized. I don't know what is wrong with her," Ponchees said to the others.

He had woken up with Gigi on his mind. She seemed distant since she found out about Sam. He wanted to see if she had said anything to Concrete and check on him. Due to their lack of communication, he didn't know how Concrete had been doing since the explosion.

"So much stuff has been going on. It is some major shit in the game. Usually, Gigi would be the person who would keep us up on what is going on with you, but something ain't right with that." Coach K said, noticing that the look in Concrete's eyes changed as soon as he said her name.

"Where is Honesty?" Concrete asked. He knew the answer to this question would solve the mystery plaguing his brain about Beautiful switching places with Gorgeous.

"We have no idea. At first, we thought she went on a trip because she had been under a lot of pressure with everything going on, but after some thought, Honesty wouldn't leave at a time like this. She is missing." Coach K said.

"So is Gigi. You all got to go and find her. That is not Gigi, that is Beautiful. She has switched places with her sister. Honesty and Gorgeous could be anywhere hurt. Beautiful has a deep-seated hate for her sister and isn't wrapped right. That girl does not have a heart." Concrete said

"I knew it, I knew!" D.J. exclaimed. His intuition never led him wrong. That is why he always made sacrifices and offerings to stay on point.

"So what in the world do we do now?" Nard asked as he looked around at the group of men.

"We need you out here with us, Concrete. What is the hold up? Why are you still in here?" Toe-Toe asked Concrete.

Tears rolled down Concrete's face. He knew that if Gigi were by his side, he would have received the best care at the top facilities. The doctors would have figured out what was going on with him. He had been in such a depression since he woke up from the explosion and found out that he could not walk. He had nobody in his corner. He felt so alone. Concrete hadn't even inquired about his treatment. He was rotting away. It was killing him that he was not going to be able to walk out of the hospital to go and search for Gigi.

"Bruh, the doctors told you that you couldn't walk?" Nard asked. He could see the anguish written all over Concrete's face. He wished he would have come and checked on him sooner.

"I had a few tests run when I first woke up. I can't feel my legs or anything. I have just been lying here in this hospital bed, miserable. Gigi is all I got. If you don't find her safe, I might as well rot to pieces. Take me from this hospital bed and put me in my grave." Concrete had promised Black Sillk on his deathbed that he would protect Gigi.

Ponchees spoke up. "Don't talk like that, son. You will be moved to a better facility before the night is over. You will have the best neurologist in the country, matter of fact, in the world. I don't care if I have to fly them here on my private plane. You will walk again, and you will see Gigi. When we find her, we are bringing her right to you. You have my word. Don't you ever say she is all you have. We are all family." He got up and went to the nurse's station to arrange to talk to whoever was in charge of Concrete's care.

"He is right. You got us, man. We got to look out for each other. Blood doesn't make you family... Loyalty does," Toe-Toe said, and he pounded fists with Concrete.

"Okay, Con, can you point us in any direction? If you were with us, where would be the first place that you would look?" Coach K was ready to hit the ground running. Time was of the essence now that the truth was out.

"She might not know that you're aware she is pretending to be her sister, so I would check the club first. She only has one friend, a

Spanish girl with two kids. Oh, and check the cemetery. She always goes to the cemetery to put flowers on Shooter's grave." Concrete said to the guys.

"Shooter? What Shooter? You talking about Jamal?" D.J. asked. He and Jamal were in boot camp and had gotten close because they were from the Westside.

Jamal came home on some other shit, robbing niggas he grew up with, and he had killed an old lady in a home invasion. They said that he was a confidential informant, and that is how he had gotten away with so many murders. Word in the street was that whoever he was informing on killed him execution-style inside the house his grand-mother had left for him when she died.

"Yeah, that was Beautiful's dude. They had been together a long time off and on since childhood." Concrete said to D.J.

Coach K was silent. That is why she was after him, because of Jamal. Beautiful had somehow found out that he was responsible for Jamal's death. She was trying to pay him back.

"We were in boot camp together, and I remember him talking about his girl. He said she was beautiful, but I didn't know that he was saying that was her name. The world is small as hell. He was my partner when we were down the road, but he came home on some fuck shit, and I came home on some get-rich shit. I do my dirt, but I don't respect a robber, especially when you are taking from the same niggas that you were in the sandbox with. His days were numbered as soon as he got home because he was slime. Don't mean to speak ill of the dead, but it's some shit you shouldn't do, and that nigga did it," D.J. said, thinking about all of the rumors he heard about Shooter. He stayed his distance because he didn't want to be affiliated with anybody like that.

"Well, looks like they were two of a kind." Coach K said aloud, but his mind was on what Concrete had told about the Spanish girl with two children. Was this a coincidence or what? No matter how he tried to stay away from Jazmeir, she kept popping up.

Chapter Thirteen

HIDE AND SEEK

Coach K felt like he was looking for a needle in a haystack. He couldn't find his daughter, and he had concluded that she had been kidnapped. He would check out the footage from the surveillance equipment he had installed when the building was broken into. He knew that some answers would be on that. As he drove toward his townhouse, his intuition told him to visit Jazmeir. After what Concrete said yesterday, he knew he had to see her. He avoided her because he didn't want his feelings to get the best of him. Even he could admit that he was in a very vulnerable state right now.

His cell phone rang, and it was a call he had been waiting for. He busted a U-turn in the middle of Northside Drive and headed toward Bankhead.

He pulled into the last carwash stall attached to the Chevron gas station, and his homie, Miami Black, approached his truck.

"Man, I swear you are the first person I called when I dropped the ten dollars on my phone card. This bad boy needs cleaning up. You got a few minutes to spare?" Miami Black got his rag from his back pocket, ready to wash Coach K's truck.

"I never have time to spare, but I always make time for you, my boy. And I always come when you call. So what's up?" Coach K reached into his pocket and handed him a five-dollar bill so he could get quarters for the car wash.

He sat beside the vacuum cleaner and watched Miami Black wash his pick-up truck. He knew he wasn't called up here for a wash, so he was patient. Even though he always gave Miami at least a hundred dollars, he didn't receive the call because he was in need.

"Word on the street is that your boy was a CI," Miami said as he sprayed the car with the hose.

All types of emotions went through Coach K's body when he heard those words. He shook his head and held it low briefly, then looked up somberly. "Say that again."

"You know my word is gospel, not gossip. My people talked about how Poke got taken down. They said he was a confidential informant. I took the first ten dollars I made and put it on the phone. I had to call you."

He kept a poker face when he responded. "Dats fucked up. Whoever he had been snitching on might have been the one to light the fire under his ass. He can't tell shit on me. I'm too legit to quit." Coach K got up and stretched his legs as he watched Miami wipe the truck to a shine. The black paint glistened like the truck was on the showroom floor.

"I know that's right, my brother. I just wanted you to know 'cause ain't no telling what other shit he was into if he had stooped that low."

"Poke had been progressed from the stooped position, he was on his belly slivering around here lately. Nothing that I'm hearing these days comes as a surprise to me where he is concerned. Have you heard anything else new...? Tell me what's going on in these streets." Coach K was fishing. He was trying to find out who could be working with Beautiful because she wasn't doing all this dirt on her lonesome. She was pulling the strings but wasn't getting her hands dirty. If Poke was gone, then it was someone who had picked up where he had left off.

Miami was wracking his brain. He heard so much different shit day in and day out up at the car wash. He tried to think of what would be helpful to Coach K. The better the info, the bigger the tip. "Oh, I heard dat slimy ass nigga May-May hit a big lick or something. He has been driving a Black Panamera; he brings it up here and gets it washed every day. You know how that goes, 'Actin' like a nigga dat ain't neva had shit.' Whatever he did, he got some good shit. But then somebody told me he got down with Gigi. But ain't Gigi your people?

The wheels in Coach K's head started to turn. Gigi knew that nigga was slime, so she wouldn't ever bring him into the fold. She hadn't said anything about getting robbed. Then it hit him: a black Panamera, the same car Beautiful drives. "Aye, where dem niggas hanging out at since they closed down Bankhead Courts?" He asked Miami as he watched him shine his tires and wheels with silicone.

Dem niggas are everywhere; they are at English Park every day in the late evening, smoking, drinking, and getting high. The majority of them ducked off into apartments that are over this way. May-May and his clique of niggas got a spot down there off Martin Luther King and Fulton Industrial in the old Suburban Court Apartments. I can't think of the name of them, but you know which ones I'm talking 'bout. But he always comes up here between five and six like clockwork."

Coach K didn't know where this info would lead him, but he knew it would help him. May-May was the type of nigga that had no morals. So, the probability that he was working for Beautiful was very high. He was a low-life, just like Poke; the only difference was that drugs didn't change his character. The nigga wasn't shit, to begin with.

He reached into his pocket, pulled out his wallet, pulled out five fifty-dollar bills, and handed them to Miami.

"I sho' appreciate this. I'm going to get me an efficiency for a week and some real rest. A brother is tired, Coach, " he said as he gratefully shook Coach K's hand.

"I'll have something else for you before the week is out. I will see you later, my dude." Coach K got into his truck, reached into his glove compartment, put his pistol on his lap, and headed to the apartment complex Miami had just told him about.

Chapter Fourteen

LIVE BY THE SWORD, DIE BY THE SWORD

Lil' Poke got off the elevator on the floor Coach K had told him that Killa was on. He couldn't believe that his best childhood friend had lost his leg and his girlfriend in a car accident. It seemed so ironic that this would be how he got injured because cars and speed were some of his first loves. He always knew that he and Killa would have something happen to them that would either hurt or take them out of the game. They both lived by the sword, so he just knew that it would be the sword that took them out. The hustle and bustle of the hospital floor resembled the emergency room, and doctors and nurses ran back and forth as he neared the room where all the commotion seemed to be coming from. There was a girl outside of the room with her head down and her shoulders shaking as she cried loudly into her hands.

He walked past the room and down the hall, looking at the room numbers on the side of all the doors. He didn't see the room number but knew he was on the correct floor. He slowed as he got to the door, where the young lady had her head down, crying loudly. He tapped her on the shoulder. "Excuse me, I'm sorry to bother you. My cousin is supposed to be in this room."

Loyalty looked up, and Lil' Poke was standing over her. "Pokey, it's me, Loyalty." She wiped her tears and running nose, then rubbed her hands down the front of her leggings.

He reached out and grabbed Loyalty in a warm embrace. She was his favorite of the three girls. If you saw Pokey and Killa, Loyalty was always somewhere close. You can see that Killa's accident took a significant toll on Loyalty. Although he hadn't seen her in person in over a year, he recognized the pain and worry on her face. "What's going on with Killa? What just happened?" he said as he peeked into the hospital room before the nurse rushed in the door and closed it behind her.

"I don't know. I just came from downstairs, getting him some magazines and snacks. He has been in and out, but he was fine when I left, and then I came back, and all hell broke out." Loyalty said as she tried to figure out what they were doing to her brother.

"Where your pops at?" Lil' Poke found it odd that Coach K was not at the hospital when his son was in distress.

"It's so much going on, and he's trying to put things together. Damn, I've been so wrapped up in my own worry I haven't called him to tell him that this happened. Stay here. I have to go downstairs because I do not have a signal up here. I will be right back." Loyalty quickly headed toward the elevator as Lil' Poke looked at her from behind.

He shook his head; Loyalty did not look like that when she and Killa came to Cali last year to visit him during the holidays. Her hips were wider, and her butt was a work of art. They are like cousins, really more like sister and brother. He shouldn't be looking at her like that, but hell, he was a man, and if he didn't look at something that looked that good without thinking twice, something was wrong with him.

The door opened, and two doctors and a nurse walked out. "Where is the young lady that was just here with the patient? I need her to get in contact with their father immediately. We need him in case the patient needs an emergency procedure." The doctor asked as he looked up and down at the young man standing suspiciously outside the door. He knew that his patient was fine when he checked on him at the beginning of his shift. He couldn't understand what had happened because his vital signs were perfect for someone his age.

"She just went to call her father. She will be right back." Lil' Poke responded with an attitude before he turned his head away from the doctor.

It seemed like too much was going on at one time, leaving him with an eerie feeling. When he went to see Beautiful, she wouldn't answer his questions. She made love to him so good it left him dizzy. She told him to come by and see her later, and she would explain everything to him, but until then, don't say anything to anybody. He didn't have anything to tell because he didn't know what was going on.

Loyalty returned, accompanied by the doctor showing her some things in Killa's chart. "My father is on his way over here. If what you and the nurse are saying is true, my brother needs to be moved immediately. I need you to have the head of security on hand when my father arrives. We will need to see the footage covering the entryways, the elevators, and the stairwells. It's a damn shame that my family isn't even safe in the fucking hospital. I need two armed security officers outside his door at all times."

Loyalty was beyond pissed. A pillow was found on the floor beside Killa's bed. Someone had tried to suffocate him. She pulled Lil' Poke by his arm and headed toward the elevator. She needed a breath of fresh air. All this was getting the best of her.

"We don't need to be leaving him up here by himself if someone just tried to take him out. What in the hell is going on around here? What do you mean you are not even safe in the hospital? You are the first person that I have seen face to face. I feel like I got on a blind-fold. I don't know what I have walked into. Please tell me." Lil' Pokey had pain etched in his eyes as he looked at Loyalty. He was hurting for Killa and Poke. He may not have been the best father, but he was still his father.

"It's like hell on Earth for us right now. It seems that we have a target on our heads. First, Honesty's spot was robbed of some bricks, our building was broken into, and Honesty's loft was trashed. Reality's truck was vandalized, and shortly after that, Gorgeous' truck was blown to pieces, and Concrete was injured as he tried to save her. Then the car accident with Killa and Leigh, the brake line was cut. Your dad and his friend get burned to death. I feel sorry for my dad 'cause he is running around like a chicken with his head cut off, trying to put the pieces together to find out who is behind all of this." As Loyalty ran down everything happening on the elevator, it hit her that she could be next.

"Damn, why didn't he call and tell me all this was going on? He didn't even call me to tell me about Killa. I thought that I was a part of this family. I would have come back home right away." Lil Poke said, filled with emotion.

"Come right home to do what? Shed more blood than what's already flowing? That's why you got sent to the West Coast to have a fresh start with new people and just be normal. I probably should have gone with you, and then I wouldn't be where I am now." She wondered if life would have been different if she'd left Atlanta after high school.

"We can't help where we come from; we were born into this life-style. This is what is flowing through our veins. You cannot stand here and honestly tell me that you didn't think that all the shit our dads have done all these years was never gonna come back to haunt them or us. Karma does not work like that. I know I have done many things in my short life, and I'm not going to question why Karma comes calling.

I'm just going to wonder when she is going to come a calling." Lil' Poke tried to put logic to how he behaved.

"Fuck that, I didn't sign up for this, and when everything is better, I'm getting the hell on. I want to go someplace where I'm not Coach K's daughter. I understand totally why Honesty left. This life can be too much for anybody." Loyalty buried her head in her hands.

Coach K walked through the hospital's automatic sliding doors with D.J., Toe-Toe and Nard bringing up the rear. He had a look of frustration and weariness written all over his face as he saw his daughter and nephew getting off the elevator. "What happened? Is everything alright?"

Loyalty rushed into her daddy's arms and rested her head on his chest. As she looked up at him with the same eyes, the tears started to pour down her face. "The doctor thinks that somebody tried to suffocate Killa."

"What in the hell?" The words loudly escaped Toe-Toe's mouth before he knew it. He started to pace back and forth, trying to calm his nerves. He really wanted to destroy something right now.

"Damn, they just letting strangers walk into the hospital and go up on the floors. How can they just have access to the patients like that? We need to talk to somebody immediately." D.J. was stunned that a private facility didn't have better security.

"This means that whomever cut his brake line is trying to finish the job. Maybe it wasn't that pussy nigga, Poke, after all." Nard said as he leaned against the wall chewing on a toothpick.

"We already know that Poke was just a puppet on her string. She got some more niggas working for her. He wasn't the only one. I'm not sparing they ass, and I'm not sparing hers either." Coach K said aloud to no one in particular.

Lil' Pokey walked closer to the four men and looked at Nard as his right temple jumped. Loyalty looked at him and she could see the flame had been ignited in him. She had often heard about how he looked when he was mad, but she'd never seen it. As he stood there, he reminded her of Killa and her dad, their temple always jumped when they were mad.

"What the fuck you mean maybe it wasn't Poke after all?"

"Calm down son, so much has been going on, I haven't been able to talk to you yet to tell you everything." Coach K reached out for Lil' Pokey.

"You got time now, you got nothing but time. Tell me why this nigga talking 'bout my pops was responsible for Killa's accident." Lil' Pokey raised his voice as he shook his arm out of Coach K's grasp. His icy stare had Nard on edge.

"First, let me see what the doctor and security have to say, then we all are going somewhere to make heads and tails of this."

Coach K was more worried about his only son than he was Lil' Pokey and his feelings. He pushed the elevator button, got on it himself, and left everyone else in the lobby.

Chapter Fifteen

"MENTION HIS NAME BRANG THE WHOLE CITY OUT!"

Coach K paced back and forth. The last thing that he wanted to do at this moment was attend Poke's funeral. He had helped plan and paid for it, and now he had to participate. Everybody expected him to be Superman at all times. His son had just lost a leg because of Poke, and now his daughter was missing. Everyone expected him to keep marching without missing a beat. Coach K was slowly unraveling. He was closer to the edge than ever, and he knew that if he were pushed over, for him to come back to the good side would be close to impossible.

The way that his heart was feeling, he couldn't care less if they put Poke's ass in an empty mason jar and tossed him off the Jackson Parkway bridge into the Chattahoochee River. But no, he couldn't let the world in on his feelings. He still had to be there for Lil' Poke, and he had to be there for Jazmeir and her kids. Poke might not have been shit at the end of his life, but he was all that they had at the end of the day. Speaking of Jazmeir, he had been avoiding her like the plague. He knew he had feelings for her; of course he did; he couldn't get her out of his mind. But she was off limits. She had a child with his mentor and was his best friend's girl.

His cell phone started to ring, and her face appeared on the screen. "Speak of the devil," he said as he hit the ignore button.

The shit was already complicated enough without him piling more stuff on. He needed Beautiful's ass under the dirt, and he needed his daughter home. That is where all his focus was now. He knew without a doubt that this would be the last public appearance that he would be making before he went underground. It's hard to hide who you are intended to be. He guessed that he had been playing the role of Coach K, the businessman, long enough, and in playing that role, people had forgotten who he was in the beginning: Crazy Coach K, the street general. More importantly, they had forgotten what he was capable of. The time had come for Crazy K to resurface, and few would be left standing in the end. He had to keep his promise to his son. His family came before everything.

Coach K slid his Armani blazer on over his sweater and grabbed his keys to head out.

––––––––––––

"I want security tripled at this funeral; spare no expense. Coach K has not been around this many people in years. Lil' Poke hasn't either. I know what Lil' Poke has been doing on the West Coast. These two men alone have a body count in the triple digits, and today will be a hard day for them. I want security there to protect them as much as I want them there to protect everybody else because they both have a temper that simmers below the surface. I can hear Coach K's voice say that he is on edge. That is why he has been staying away. But I know him well enough to be able to tell just by talking to him. Lil' Poke is more like Coach K than his own son; he sent him away because he knew what damage he could do if he were to stay in Atlanta." Ponchees laid in the bed naked from the waist up in his place of residence whenever he was in Atlanta, the Presidential Suite at the Ritz Carlton in Buckhead.

Sam walked around the suite in her bra and boy shorts. She was tired and wanted to stay in, but she knew Ponchees was not attending the funeral, so she had to be there to be his eyes and ears. She had not been sleeping well the last three days. As if things couldn't get worse, her brother had popped up like a jack in the box, like always, asking her for a favor. Then, on top of everything else, she had a positive pregnancy test yesterday. The last thing that she needed to be doing was getting pregnant by a sixty-five-year-old man who didn't have any kids.

She wanted to scream at the top of her lungs; at least, that is what her first mind told her. But her second mind was telling her to get as much money as she could grab and get the hell on, disappear. This would be easy as hell if her boyfriend were not one of the chiefs of the Mexican cartel or maybe if her brother wasn't a special agent in the FBI. Just the thought of it gave her a migraine as she slipped on the navy blue collared shirtdress.

Sam looked over at Ponchees lying in the bed, and she knew that even if she could, she wouldn't leave this man. She walked over to the walk-in closet, reached for the shelf, and pulled out one of the many shopping bags that carried some of the things he had purchased for her the day before. He knew that spending money on her always stopped her from being mad at him, especially when he actually went shopping with her, watched her try on the clothes, and gave her suggestions.

"Everything is going to be fine, Papi. I got everything set up, and I'm going to call them again as soon as I get in the car to make sure they have swept the funeral home for weapons." Sam sat on the edge of the bed and put on a pair of red designer wedges. She then leaned back, and Ponchees leaned forward and kissed her deeply.

He knew that Sam could handle herself as well as the operation. He didn't mean to chastise her in front of everyone else, but he was sure that the twenty thousand dollars he spent at Phipps Plaza yesterday made her feel better.

As she walked out the door, her conversation with her brother replayed in her head.

"Sam, I need to know where Poke's body is and where the funeral is being held. How does his family expect people to come to the funeral if it's not public knowledge where it's being held? Anyway, that's on them; I need to go in. I need to place a few men in there to see who all is coming and going."

"Deon, you are the FBI; you are supposed to know everything about every-body. Why are you asking about Poke, he was just a junky? Them folks weren't making no noise." Sam's heart was pounding. *Poke wasn't making any noise now, but he was affiliated with some real noisemakers.*

"Calm down, lil' sister. Poke was one of our people. He has been for the past year. I just wanna see who is gonna show up. He wasn't shit, but if you mention his boy Coach K's name, the city is bound to come out."

It seemed like all the air left Sam's body when her brother said Poke was a confidential informant. How did that get past her? How much had he told her brother about Gigi, Ponchees, and Coach K before he was murdered? This still seemed unreal to her as she thought of a way out. The last thing she needed was for Ponchees to find out that her brother was an FBI agent. He wouldn't forgive her, even if she had been the one doing things all these years to keep the Feds off of him. She was the reason that they were flying under the radar despite the large amount of dope that Ponchees had trafficked into the country every week.

———

Jazmeir looked at the picture of her and Poke on their last vacation. They had gone to the Dominican Republic; he wanted to see her home. Things were so good for them then, and they looked so happy. Poke wasn't always the bad guy to her. He was caring and he encouraged her dreams. He had good intentions. He just got lost along the way. When she told him that she wanted to decorate for a living, the first thing he asked her was what he needed to do to make her dream come true. Poke didn't know that she had her own money. All he knew was that her baby's father had died, and before she got with him, she was a stripper. Poke just kept telling her that he was not going to let her go back into the strip club and that he would do anything possible to make sure that she didn't.

The sadness from losing Black Sillk was still apparent when they first got together. She was in mourning for the man who was like sunshine to her and made her thoughts of the future bright. Jazmeir wore black every day and barely wanted to leave the house. It was hard to tell if she was going through postpartum depression or just in mourning. The days and nights ran together, and the only thing keeping her from slipping into oblivion was her newborn son.

The baby that she had just given birth to would never get to meet his dad; she would never get to marry the man she loved, who saved her from a life of demeaning herself by stripping for a living. Her solemn mood was quickly replaced with happiness once her sister came to the States. She reminded her she had so much to live for, including the handsome milk chocolate little boy with a head full of black silky curls. She named him Champion because she was sick from the beginning, and miscarriage had been a threat throughout her entire pregnancy. Now, her son was the spitting image of his father and her pride and joy.

It wasn't long before her sister met a guy herself and fell in love. He was murdered a month before she died, giving birth to her daughter. They left a newborn daughter behind for Jazmeir to raise. Poke came along and helped her to heal from Black Sillk and her sister's passing.

He was all she had, except for the two children and Beautiful, who was frequently in and out of town. She had gotten used to not having her around at all.

Jazmeir's heart wasn't heavy because of Poke's passing. She was hurt because of the way that he died. He was burnt alive, and no one deserved to die that way. She had just gotten used to people around her dying. Her parents died at a young age, and then her grandmother lost her battle with breast cancer, Black Sillk, and then her sister. Jazmeir felt that she was just numb to death. It was okay to be sad and to grieve, but she couldn't mourn because she still had two kids to take care of.

The knock at the door startled her out of her reverie. She opened the door, and the limo driver was there to take her to the funeral. Coach K had insisted that she come to the funeral in a limo because she was Poke's family. She remembered when she thought the same. Jazmeir put her hat on her head and lowered her veil as she prepared to go to the funeral of the last man who would ever break her heart.

Chapter Sixteen

DRESSED IN ALL BLACK LIKE THE OMEN

Sam could tell as she pulled up at Raleigh Rucker's funeral home that although this funeral hadn't been publicized as a typical funeral would be, with obituaries in the newspapers, it had still brought out many people. There was no processional from the family home, but the parking lot was filled with every exotic car you could think of, parked right beside the hoopties. She could already imagine what was taking place inside the chapel. She took a deep breath, leaned against the car, and looked toward the sky. Today was definitely going to be a hell of a day.

Rafek walked up to his boss with his head down. He knew she was still upset with him because she only responded with short answers and barely looked at him in his eyes. He had to make it up to her. He would, but for now, his first job was to protect her. "So what's first on the agenda?" He asked as he shifted from one foot to the other and put his hands in the pocket of his slacks.

"Nigga, today is not going to be a good day, so quit with the long face. Apologize so that I can accept. We got bigger fish to fry, and that's the frying pan right there." Sam pointed at the building in front of them with the double RRs on the front of it.

A smile crept across Rafek's face; this was easier than he thought. "I'm sorry for everything that happened, and I promise that it isn't going to happen again. I got your back when nobody does." He bent his tall, thick frame and hugged Sam tightly, picking her up off the ground.

"Boy, put me down, and let's make sure everything is in place." Sam swatted Rafek's arm as she put her arm in his and they walked toward the armed security parking in the black SUV parked on side of the chapel. She knew that she needed to be called out on her bullshit sometimes, and she was used to Ponchees doing it. But when Rafek did it, it hit a sore spot with her.

The limos pulled up slowly as the steady stream of people poured into the chapel dressed in their finest threads. It looked more like the hip-hop awards versus a funeral; all that was missing was the red carpet. Women stepped lightly in towering heels and tight dresses as the men stepped hard in the same designer shoes. Repeatedly, they gave hugs, pounds, and fake air kisses to people they otherwise prob-ably wouldn't even bat an eyelid at. This was the new culture in Atlanta; it was hard to tell the real from the fake, and the social networking sites had made everybody friends.

Lil' Poke stepped out of the Audi R8 he had rented to drive during his stay in Atlanta. Coach K had urged him to ride in the limo with Jazmeir, but he decided against it. He had yet to meet his so-called stepmother, and he didn't want to feel awkward on the ride over. In actuality, he needed time to get his thoughts together. Lil' Poke was old enough to know better. His father was never the most stand-up guy in the world, but the things he had found out about him since he had been back in Atlanta were hard to fathom. It took everything in him not to wild out at the hospital on Nard for being reckless with his mouth. He knew that his father had not been the reason for Killa's accident. He thought that he had come back to bury his father, but now it seemed as if he was going to have to clear his name as well.

Coach K nodded to the people as he tried quickly getting into the chapel. He didn't want to talk to anyone. He just wanted to be in and out. His mind was not on Poke now; Poke was dead and gone. He was focused on Beautiful and finding his daughter. He went to the front row reserved for family and was the first to sit down. He put his head into his hands. The stress of the world around him was taking its toll on him. Killa was at home under the care of an in-home nurse and doctor. Loyalty didn't want to leave her brother's side, so she decided against attending the funeral. She still hadn't revealed to her father that she was pregnant by K.J., and he still hadn't revealed to her his connection to K. J. He wanted to get up right then as the tears fought to come out of his eyes as he thought about the fact that his oldest daughter could be somewhere hurt or even worse.

Coach K got up from the pew and went to find Rucker. He needed this service to start immediately so he could look for his daughter.

Reality and D.J. sat down right as Coach K was getting up. He put his hand up to signal that he would be right back as he walked toward a side door in the front of the chapel. D.J. grabbed Reality's hand in his. He knew she was on edge; she had been tossing and turning in their bed for the last two nights. He felt they were not doing enough to find Honesty and get Beautiful. It seemed like everybody had the same agenda, but no one was taking action. They had unlimited resources, but everybody was so caught up in their emotions that they did nothing to solve the problem. Maybe it was like that because it was family involved. He wasn't family and planned on doing something today before anyone stopped him.

The music started to play just as Jazmeir walked through the chapel door. She was dressed in black from head to toe, except for the red-bottomed heels on her feet. The veil hid her face as she kept her eyes pointed straight ahead. Her hands sweated inside the red lace gloves.

She was nervous. She would meet Poke's son for the first time; she had only talked to him over the phone as they discussed the arrangements. She would also be seeing Coach K. He seemed so preoccupied lately. He wouldn't tell her what was going on with him and kept his conversation very basic whenever she asked him about anything outside of Poke. Jazmeir's heart sped up at the thought of him. She knew she was not supposed to think of him like this, and although she tried not to, she couldn't help herself.

Life-sized pictures of Poke lined the front of the chapel, displaying him in his happier times. One was of him, Jazmeir, and the kids, one of him and his grandmother with Lil' Poke at his high school graduation, and one with him, Coach K, and Black Sillk that was taken at the Players' Ball years ago.

Coach K and Rucker came back through the side door. Coach K sat in the front row with his daughter, Reality, and Jazmeir. A slide show of pictures of Poke throughout the years played on the giant screen as Raleigh Rucker cleared his throat to get everyone's attention.

At that moment, the sanctuary doors burst open loudly as Lil' Poke walked in. The CD playing softly seemed to scratch, and the melody skipped as everyone watched him walk in. He had been off the scene for almost three years, had gotten taller and leaner, and looked like a grown man. His shadow beard was trimmed perfectly on his face, blending well with his jet-black temped afro. His thick, curly hair glistened under the lights and the jewels he wore. The whispers escalated to murmurs as Handsome walked in behind him, and they fell into step, walking down the aisle, their strides matching step by step. If you didn't know them, you would think they were brothers. They were the same height, had the same curly hair and cut, and even had the same mouth.

Rucker cleared his throat again to gain the attention of the overly packed sanctuary. He had been talking to Coach K lately, so he knew what path Poke was on before his death; this made it hard for him to eulogize him. He had started jotting down notes and drew a blank. He was trying to rewind his mind to the Poke, who always had a joke, a smile, or a young girl on his arm. "Thank you, gentlemen, for joining us. I would like to start the service now. We are all gathered here to pay tribute to Abdullah Ibrahim, affectionately known by most of us as Slow Poke. A friend, a loving father, and someone well-known in the community." He took a deep breath because Poke was also a murderer, a womanizer, and a robber, to say the least.

Rucker had brought in some professional mourners because he knew no one would be sad or show empathy at this funeral. He looked up from the podium at the audience of stoic faces staring at him, waiting for him to give them words of comfort.

"Poke was a character. He always had a story to tell that would leave you bent over in laughter. I'm sure you all can remember those stories that Poke used to tell. Before I moved to this location, I was on the Westside with McCray all the time, and Poke and K would sit up at the funeral home with us. One night, it was late, and it was storming outside. We were playing cards and suddenly heard noises coming from the back. The back is where all the bodies were stored, and the embalming took place. Poke jumped up, pulled his gun from his waistband, and pointed it toward the back where the noise was coming from. The rest of us had not moved a lick. He looked at us like we were crazy because we were not moving, nor were we alarmed. The creaking noise seemed to be getting louder, but it didn't appear to be coming closer; then, suddenly, there was a crash and big boom, and then Poke started emptying the clip down the dark hallway. To make a long story short, a gigantic tree limb had broken off over the funeral home and smashed through the roof. McCray jumped up finally, looked Poke dead in the eyes, and said, 'I ain't never seen a gangster try to kill some dead people again.' And we all burst into laughter."

Rucker looked at the crowd, and the mood lightened as the crowd laughed at his story. He knew to quit while he was ahead. "I'm not going to bore you all with all my Poke stories; I would like to give you, his loved ones, a few minutes to share with us what he meant to you. I know Poke put a smile on all of our faces. Please limit your remarks to three minutes. " He breathed a sigh of relief as he stepped away from the podium.

Coach K sat in his seat, stone-faced, thinking about what he would say. He knew people were expecting him to say something; he hated to say that, which is why many people attended the funeral. Sweat poured down his face and neck as he felt the eyes of the crowd boring into him from behind. He rubbed his sweaty palms down the front of his slacks as he scooted to the edge of the pew and prepared to get up. Just as he took a deep breath and stood up, Lil' Poke walked up the three steps to approach the microphone at the podium.

"It's good to see all of you here today. For whatever reason you decided to come, I thank you. Now, I'm not about to get up here and sing all of my father's praises. He was Slow Poke to you; he was Slow Poke to me, too. I never called him dad or pops, and he didn't force me to. He wasn't perfect, but I guess he cared for me the best he could. He could've left me outside when my mother left me on his doorstep when I was only a few days old. He raised me, and while he didn't teach me everything firsthand, I learned through his mistakes. I'm thankful for that. Many people don't realize that you can actually learn from other people's mistakes. We do not have to follow the beaten path. We aren't always meant to be a chip off the old block. I mean, why would you want to be a chip off the old block if the block wasn't hitting on shit? So I say to you, be better than your circumstance, and I say to Slow Poke, thank you for taking me in, and thank you for being a big fuck up so I can be a real man." Lil' Poke looked out at the crowd of people one last time, and into the eyes of Coach K. Then he stepped away from the podium and walked straight out of the chapel doors.

Murmurs went through the crowd as they talked about what Lil' Poke had just said. Everyone was in shock. Rucker was, too, as he signaled to the gospel singer Diana Nicole to start singing. Her beautiful voice filled the chapel as she laid out a soulful rendition of "Tell Him" by Lauryn Hill. There wasn't a dry eye in the building when she made it to the second verse. She had made the song her own.

Coach K got up and followed Lil' Poke. He had to go and console him. He knew that he was in a lot of pain right now. He was proud of what he had said, but he knew it was only a snippet of what was happening inside him. He wasn't worried about what he would do if pushed over the edge; he needed to be worried about if Lil' Poke had already toppled over the edge.

Toe-Toe, Nard, and Mom-Dukes were sitting in the last pew in the back of the chapel. They all look at each other with the same shock on everybody else's face. They got up and walked out behind Coach K.

Tears flowed down Jazmeir's face, and a loud cry erupted from her suddenly as the singer's melodic voice flowed into the song's last verse. She remembered telling the funeral home director to find a singer to sing a non-denominational song that spoke of a higher power because she didn't want to offend anyone's religious beliefs. The song shook her to the core. It made her think about Black Sillk. She couldn't stop the tears from falling, and as she tried to stop crying loudly and compose herself, she seemed to get louder. She was never one to display her emotions, but that song made her think of Black Sillk and Coach K. Slow Poke never entered her mind as she got up from the pew and walked out of the chapel so fast that she almost lost her footing as she reached the double doors just as the singer was closing the song.

Rucker stood up as she was finishing the song. He looked into the audience for the young lady he had talked to earlier in the week about the extra security. After what he had just seen, he was sure that something else fucked up was bound to happen. He decided to end the service right then. He informed everyone of the repast Coach K had arranged at the Exclusive event space. He had already paid for 300 people to eat and drink for the next four hours to celebrate the life of his old best friend.

Chapter Seventeen

WHY DON'T YOU LOVE ME?

Jazmeir's heart pounded fast as she approached Lil' Poke and Coach K standing outside. She didn't know what to say or what to do. The song was replaying over and over in her head. *Tell him I love him, tell him I need him, it will be alright.* Right now, she just felt so alone, and she knew that the only person alive who could take that feeling away was Coach K. She could tell that they were deep in conversation. As Coach K embraced Lil' Poke, she could see that he loved the young man. Jazmeir knew that Poke was always envious of his son's relationship with Coach K. She remembered him telling her how everyone treated Coach K like a king, including his own son.

As she watched the two men standing there, she noticed a resemblance. Maybe it was because they had been around each other for so long. She took a deep breath as she stood silently, waiting for them to acknowledge her. Lil' Poke was the first to look at her, and his intense stare startled her a little, but what had her even more shaken was that his eyes looked just like Coach K's.

"Sorry if that isn't what you were expecting. I hope I didn't ruin my father's homegoing service for you. I know that you put a lot into planning this. I didn't plan on saying that, but that is what came out, and I'm okay with it. I appreciate you taking on the bulk of this funeral's responsibility. I don't think I could've done it." Lil' Poke walked over to Jazmeir as she took her hat off. Her beauty left him speechless as she hugged him. He looked over her head as she embraced him and looked at Coach K, who was watching her with a peculiar look, one that Lil' Poke couldn't quite put his finger on.

"I am happy that I was able to help. Your father meant a lot to me. He wasn't always the bad guy. He helped lift me up when I was at my lowest, so I will always be grateful." Jazmeir locked hands with Lil' Poke when their embrace ended, but she couldn't take her eyes off Coach K. She wanted to be in his arms.

Lil' Poke knew that Jazmeir was younger than his father, but she looked to be his age. He thought to himself, *Damn Pop was robbing the cradle.* She sounded young on the phone, but the things she spoke of made her seem older and much more mature than someone his age.

The chapel doors opened, and a few people started to pour out. Coach K recognized Toe-Toe, Nard, and Mom-Dukes coming their way. He walked toward them. He was excited to see his old friend. He grabbed her tightly and hugged her. She reminded him of the good ole days. He could picture them sitting in Beloved's living room, listening to the record player and smoking joints. "Girl, look at you, still looking the same. Thank you for coming. I need your boys to bring you to the house to catch up. I got to take care of a lot of business, but you all go over to repast and enjoy yourself. Everything is on me."

"I'm going to go ahead and dip out before everyone else comes out. There is no use in being fake. I paid my last respects to my father, so my job as a son is done. It was nice meeting you. Thank you again." Lil' Poke pulled away from Jazmeir and started to walk toward his car.

A black Yukon with dark tinted windows came speeding around the corner with the windows down. Masked men hung out the window with guns and started to let loose. Lil' Poke instantly dived on top of Jazmeir.

Toe-Toe pulled out his pistol and started to run while busting at the truck. Nard dove on top of his mother to shield her from the bullets that seemed to be coming directly toward them. Coach K had been hit with a hail of gunfire from the automatic weapons, and he lay on the ground bleeding with his eyes closed, right next to Nard and Mom-Dukes.

Lil' Poke got up off Jazmeir as the gunfire stopped, and as soon as she looked over and saw Coach K on the ground, a scream pierced the air. "Oh my God, Noooooooooooo!"

Chapter Eighteen

LEAVING

Honesty was so tired, and her arms and fingers were numb from trying to get untied from the chair. She didn't know how much time had passed since Gigi had been shot, but she knew that her breathing had changed, and she was no longer moaning. She had to get free so that she could save their lives. Honesty closed her eyes briefly and then looked up and prayed as she tried to pull her hand through the rope she had managed to loosen. She yanked her right hand so hard it felt like she had pulled her shoulder out of the joint. The pain went through her as she was able to twist her body around and untie the other hand. As she bent down to take the tape off her ankles, she heard a low moan from Gigi.

As soon as Honesty got the last piece of tape from around her ankles, she stood up and collapsed within the same few seconds. She was weak from sitting in the same place and not eating for all those hours. Her legs were like spaghetti, but she willed them to work because her strength was their only hope of survival. Honesty crawled a few feet to where Gigi was lying, her eyes barely open.

Her breathing was so shallow, and inside, Honesty was scared she wouldn't make it. She looked down and saw that Gigi's shirt was saturated with blood. She was scared to move her, but she cradled her head. She had lost a lot of blood. The bullet hole was in her lower abdomen, and the blood had pooled around her.

"Baby, can you hear me? I'm right here. I don't want to leave you, but I have to get you some help. Say something, baby. Please let me know that you are alright." Tears poured down Honesty's face and landed on Gigi's cheek. She looked up at her.

Honesty had been in and out of it, so she didn't even know how long they had been in the warehouse. Her head throbbed, and her body hurt, but she gently placed Gorgeous' head back down. She stood up on her wobbly legs and headed toward the window. She looked out, and instantly, she knew exactly where they were.

"Don't leave me. I'm scared," Gigi uttered painfully. She closed her eyes. The cold feeling was taking over her body. She remembered when the bullet first hit her, she felt like she was on fire. Now, she wished she could feel the heat.

Honesty rushed back over to her side and knelt. She rubbed her head. Seeing Gorgeous like this tore her apart, but she had to do something to get her to a hospital. "I know where we are. We are right here by Whitehall Street. If I could walk out and find somebody with a cell phone, I could call the paramedics."

"I'm so cold, I'm so cold." Gigi's teeth chattered as she used her energy to get Honesty to stay with her. She didn't want to die alone. It wasn't her time yet. There were so many things that she had not done yet.

"I got to go and get help, baby. Just stay with me. I promise I will be right back." Honesty held Gorgeous and smoothed her hair down soothingly. She wanted her to stay calm. The last thing she needed was for her to go into shock.

Gorgeous lay on the floor. Her body was so cold she felt like she was in Antarctica. She knew she had angels looking out for her, and she was calling on all of them. This could not be the way that she would die, on the floor in a rat-infested warehouse in her piss and blood. She had to go out better than that; she figured she had paid enough dues to at least die in dignity.

Her mind raced as she thought about the time she found her aunt dead in her bed when she was a little girl and how Sillk had died at home in his bed peacefully. She hoped she had sown enough seeds of goodness to be blessed with a peaceful death.

Chapter Nineteen

REMEMBER EVERYBODY AIN'T LOYALTY

Loyalty's father had told her to listen out for the new doctor and nurse coming over. Her brother had come home with a doctor and a nurse, but her father didn't feel comfortable with the older black man. His healing methods seem to be a little outdated. She just hoped whoever he chose was a good doctor because seeing her brother like this was killing her inside. She thought him losing his leg was the worst of his battle.

Coach K had gone to the hospital administrator, adamant that his son receive the best care. He threatened to sue them because of the lack of security, and the medical director insisted on sending his son home with the top rehabilitation specialist in Atlanta. The older gray-haired gentleman came to his house and did his best, but he didn't fit the family well. Coach K returned to the hospital and told the medical director to send him the next in line and ensure they were younger than fifty years old.

The doorbell rang just as Loyalty finished a timed quiz on her iPad for school. Despite everything going on, she had not fallen behind in her schoolwork. Her stomach growled loudly as she picked up her pistol from her purse and walked through the den toward the front door. She had forgotten to eat today. As she gently rubbed her stomach with her other hand, she reminded herself that she was now eating for two.

Loyalty opened the door, and standing before her was the doctor who had tried to pay for her snacks that day in the hospital. Her first instinct was to shut the door, run into the powder room, freshen up, and then open the door again. She knew she couldn't do that, so she opened the door and leaned into the doorjamb with her pistol in her right hand. Her left hand went to her hair; she knew it looked a mess. She probably hadn't run a comb through it in at least a month.

"Is this the Rasheed residence?" the doctor said, flashing a smile. Butterflies swept into his stomach as soon as he saw Loyalty's face. He didn't know where the medical director was sending him; he just told him to pick his best nurse and that he would be compensated very nicely.

"Yes, it is. You must be the doctor that I've been expecting. Where is your nurse?" Loyalty said as she moved out of the doorjamb and let the doctor in. She noticed his Audi A8 parked behind her truck in the driveway.

"Yes, I'm Dr. Aidan Ryan. My nurse will be coming in later. She is flying back into Atlanta from Washington D.C." He said as he looked her up and down as they stood in the foyer. Even with the pistol at her side, she was beautiful. Now, he would have the chance to get to know the young lady who had sparked his interest.

Loyalty felt flustered, but she blamed it on the fetus growing inside of her as she led the doctor through the den to the bedroom where Killa was situated. The extra-large hospital bed that her father had ordered made her brother look like a child. He was hooked up to all the machines, and the room was dimly lit, with Ken Ford playing softly in the background. She wanted the atmosphere to be calming because she didn't know what was going on in his sleep or what battles he was fighting that were making his blood pressure spike.

The doctor immediately went to Killa's bedside, took out his stethoscope, and checked his vitals. He then picked up his chart from the nightstand and looked at the last notes that the previous doctor had written. The doctor's handwriting was horrible, but he understood the shorthand. He was stable and had not spiked a fever within the last forty-eight hours.

Loyalty sat back down on the oversized leather chaise lounge. She watched the doctor as he read the notes from the previous doctor and checked her brother out. She still felt the butterflies, the same ones that she felt that night in the hospital when he tried to buy her stuff in the gift shop. He was handsome and successful, but he was white. Loyalty had never been with a white man. They flirted with her; some even asked her out, but she never gave them the time of day.

"Umm hmm, um hmmm," he cleared his throat, trying to get the attention of the beautiful lady staring into space.

"Yes, I'm sorry. Did I miss something?" Loyalty said as she tucked her legs under her and sat Indian-style on the chaise.

"My God, could you be more beautiful? I'm sorry, I'm sorry. Please forgive me. What was I about to say?" His thoughts were scrambled, and he was at a loss for words. But he had to admit, she was breathtaking.

Loyalty blushed at the compliment from the doctor. Just when she thought she was looking her worst. She was barely washing her face, much less her ass these days. She had looked in the mirror earlier; she had dark circles under her eyes, and her face looked hollow because she had not been eating. But he said that she was beautiful. She peeked at him under her naturally long lashes, trying to hide her smile. "If you think I'm beautiful now, you should see me after I've had a bath and some rest." Loyalty laughed for the first time in months.

The doctor looked over at her sleeping brother and back at her. They actually looked just alike. "Are you and your brother twins? I'm not saying he is beautiful, but I just noticed you have all the same features and complexion."

"We might as well be. We are the same age and look alike but don't have the same mother." Loyalty got up from the chaise, walked over to the other side of her brother's bed, rubbed his face, and ran her hand through his hair. She hated to see him suffering. It was taking a toll on her, along with her heartbreak. She knew that when all this was over, she would go away for a while to get herself together. There was only so much a person could take.

"You got to be kidding me! Well, your father sure has some strong genes. I'm going to start to wean him off this medication. He is a healthy young man, and I don't need him lying up medicated when he could be up and around, living his life. As soon as he is fully conscious and can talk to me about his pain tolerance, I will be ready to start his next course of treatment. His nurse is going to be a big help. She is an expert in cases like his. We were stationed together in Afghanistan, and she is credited for awesome therapy methods." The doctor kept looking at the young man so he wouldn't drown his sister's dark, doe-like eyes.

"That sounds great. I'm ready for him to be back on his feet. We will spare no expense to get Killa back to one hundred percent. I know my father wants the best money can get him. I wish he could be ready for our graduation in a few months." Loyalty wanted her and her brother to walk across that stage together to get their bachelor's degrees.

"You never know. It all really depends on your brother. Rehab is one hundred percent a mind thing. His mind has to tell his body what to do. I have seen some men who lie down after an amputation and wallow in self-pity. They don't want to do anything. They get bedsores. Then I have seen some people get their new limbs and look at it as what it is, another chance at life. They thrive because they are just happy they get another chance at life. Sometimes, these injuries are just a wake-up. Especially in your brother's case, he is like my men in Afghanistan. They might be the only person that survived a bombing. The fact that they got a second chance is like an awakening. They are never the same." The doctor was thinking about his nurse, who was about to join him on this assignment. She had lost her leg in a bombing, and on her first day with her prosthesis, she was damn near running. The nurse wanted to help all of the injured soldiers even more after she was injured herself.

Loyalty hoped her brother was one of the ones who looked at it as another chance for a better life. Killa had done a lot of wrong in his short life. Maybe this accident will finally make him leave that street life alone. As her father said, this would turn him into a saint or a beast.

"Well, Ms. Rasheed, I will be back tomorrow. My nurse should be coming in around nightfall. I have already informed her that she will do twelve hours daily. I know your brother doesn't want her fawning over him and in his face all the time, so your father arranged for her to have space in one of your guest rooms. He informed me that you had been doing most of the work regarding being your brother's caregiver, so this should relieve you." The doctor said, finally looking Loyalty in her eyes.

"I have had no problem taking care of my brother. He would be right by my side if the roles were reversed. However, I can handle some things I have neglected with the nurse on duty. My main concern is my brother."

"He is in good hands now. Please give us some of your burden. That is what we are here for." The doctor saw the pain in Loyalty's eyes. If helping her brother to walk again would take that look away, he was willing to do whatever he had to do. There was something special about this young lady; he would find out what it was sooner or later.

Chapter Twenty

ABG- ANYBODY GET IT!

"Right now, I don't trust no fucking one. Anyone can get it, and everybody is a got damn suspect!" Coach K said through clenched teeth as he looked at the group gathered around his hospital bed.

"Calm down. We are on top of it. Everything is going to be resolved." Ponchees said as he looked at his old friend with his arm in a sling and a bandage around his head.

"I can't continue to keep calm when all this shit is falling apart around me. The Coach K everyone knew of died in the parking lot of Raleigh Rucker's Funeral Home. The old Coach K is back, and there is hell to pay; that is the only currency I accept. Hell, for all that I have been involved in and everything that has taken place with my family these last three months, and if anyone in this room has been a part of it, trust and believe you will be seeing hell sooner than later."

Coach K. had just woke up from surgery to remove the bullet from his shoulder. He looked around, and it was like he had died in the parking lot for real because now he trusted no one. Ponchees, Sam, Lil' Poke, D.J.. Nard, Toe-Toe, Reality, and Jazmeir were all there when he woke up, but he woke up feeling alone because the last face he saw before he blacked out was Beloved.

"Pop's, just let Uncle Ponchees handle everything. You know he has a far reach." Reality moved to her father's bedside and grabbed his other hand. She didn't want to lose her father in this battle. His determination was fierce, but she wanted him to hand the baton to someone else because if he had died in the parking lot, it would've shattered her, and she would never be the same.

Jazmeir looked at him sadly as many emotions ran through her. She had passed out in the parking lot at the thought that she might have lost Coach K. There was so much more that she had to experience in her life, and she wanted to experience with him. She promised herself that as soon as she had time alone with him, she would tell him exactly how she felt. Her soft voice sounded like that of a child. "Please, just recover from your injuries and let Ponchees handle everything, Coach K."

Coach K' sat upright in the bed, gritting his teeth and closing his eyes as the pain shot through him from the sudden motion. "Everybody keep hollering, let Ponchees handle it, let Ponchees handle it! Well I tried that! Ponchees is not taking this shit seriously enough. His blood is not being spilled, and his family is not being hurt. If Ponchees were handling things, my son would not be at home with one leg, Leigh and Poke wouldn't be dead, Concrete wouldn't be in the hospital, and my daughter wouldn't be out there, God knows where. I can no longer put my family's well-being in his hands."

Ponchees felt the dagger shoot straight to his heart as the words that came from Coach K's mouth penetrated him. He knew that he was right. Ponchees had let Sam handle everything, and in the midst of her handling everything, she had not handled anything at all. Surveillance was supposed to be in place, which would have given them the one-up on everything going on with Poke if he was indeed the culprit. It would also let them know everyone that Poke had been in contact with. He would not scold her in front of anyone again, but he would get to the bottom of everything. Sam's hand was intertwined with his; he squeezed her fingers tightly to let her know that he was beyond pissed.

Sam didn't know if it was her pregnancy or what, but she exploded. "Have you ever thought about what would've happened thus far if you didn't have the extra eyes and ears in the city that belong to me? I'm not God, and I have been keeping the outsiders off your ass. I can't help you when your friends are your worst foes. That's your mother-fucking fault. Miss me with all the bullshit, trust and believe, without me it could have been a hell of a lot worse." She ripped her hand from Ponchees' grasp and walked out the hospital room door with tears running down her face. She could not believe they were making her seem like the bad guy. She needed to get back to her office to gather her thoughts and get to the bottom of this. She might just need her big brother's help.

Ponchees thought about it, and Sam was right in a way. He kept the outsiders out, but the insiders did the most damage to this family. There was no way Coach K should be lying in this hospital bed. He had security at the funeral home. Why weren't they on their job? Everything goes back to him, leaving everything in Sam's hands. He rubbed his hand through his thick salt and pepper mane in frustration. "I promise I will get to the bottom of this if this is the last thing I do." He patted his friend on his good shoulder and left the hospital room to go after Sam.

Coach K pulled the I.V. out of his arm. He looked over to Lil' Poke. "Get my clothes out of the bag. I'm going home. I got to find my daughter and make sure that Gigi is alright. This bitch, Beautiful is at the bottom of this, and I don't give a damn who she is related to; this bitch has to die. I don't care if I die killing her. None of this shit should've fucking happened. None of it!" he shouted, scaring everyone in the room.

Lil' Poke stood still for a brief second, then he reached and picked up the neatly folded stack of clothes that Reality had brought for her dad. The clothes that he wore to the funeral had been cut off him. He was torn; his first mind said that he had to have Coach K's back no matter what because he had always been there for him, but his heart told him that he needed to protect Beautiful because she was the only woman that had ever been in his heart.

Chapter Twenty-One

RIDING THROUGH MY OLD HOOD, BUT I'M IN MY NEW WHIP

Beautiful couldn't risk being seen at Poke's funeral. She had May-May doing her dirty work, so she was waiting for the phone call to let her know everything was done. She probably shouldn't have gone to the warehouse, but she did, and now her sister and Honesty were out of the way. All she had to do now was hear that Coach K was out of the picture. Everything would be smooth sailing from here on out because she knew that Ponchees would pick up and return to Mexico, or at least she hoped so.

Her heart beat out of control as her mind raced. She had finally done something she had been dreaming about doing for a long time. She had eliminated Gorgeous.

The adrenaline raced through her veins, and she felt a high unlike any high that she had ever felt before, and God knows, with all the drugs that she had done over the years, that she had felt some highs.

When she set Poke's house on fire, she felt satisfied, but this feeling was way more than satisfaction. With her sister behind her, she would be able to live her life as she was destined to, on top of the world.

The full moon lit the sky as she drove aimlessly with the sunroof open, allowing the fall air to flow through the black-on-black Rolls Royce. Beautiful had come a long way from her days as a loner living in the Carrie Steele Pitts group home.

She used to cut school daily and go to Bankhead Courts to hang out and get high. Now, as she drove through the Westside, hardly anything looked familiar. All the projects she once hung out in were either rebuilt or just fields of grass and trees.

Beautiful ended up on Perry Blvd before she knew it. The car seemed to be on autopilot as she turned the ignition off in front of her old building. This was the only place she had ever called her home. This was her first and last home.

So many thoughts ran through her mind as she wondered why Solitaire couldn't have been a regular mother. Why did she choose the streets and drugs over her three children? Why couldn't she be more like Gorgeous? Why had nobody ever loved her? And why did Big Man do that to her?"

She laid her head on the steering wheel and wept loudly as visions of her sister standing over Big Man with the butcher knife in his back flooded her mind. She would never forget all the blood then, and now her shooting her sister and all the blood. Her sister had saved her life. She'd killed for her; she couldn't leave her dying in a dirty, deserted warehouse.

Beautiful lifted her head and started the car. She had to go back to help her sister. Their grandmother was probably turning over in her grave.

"Fuck that lil' ungrateful bitch, let her die. You are right where you belong now. You are on top. Did you ever think that you would finally get rid of her? If you were somewhere dying, she wouldn't come and save you. Let her bleed to death. You got everything that you dreamed of. If you go back there, you will end up scraping the bottom of the barrel as usual." Solitaire's voice was filled with malice.

Beautiful wiped the tears away. "You're right, mommy. I am supposed to be on top, not her. I did what you wanted me to do. I'm going to make you proud, I promise.

"Now is the time for you to shine like a diamond. You are not finished yet." Solitaire encouraged her daughter.

Beautiful blinked hard to clear her vision. She pulled down at the mirror to see her reflection. Make-up was smeared across her face. Her mother was gone now. She knew she was special, just like her mother always said. That's why her mother and Jamal came to visit her all the time. Now, she had to figure out what she was going to do. She couldn't go back to the warehouse.

Gorgeous was bound to bleed to death eventually, and Honesty was still tied up so she would starve to death. She didn't want to return to her place because it was so close to the warehouse. But she didn't know where to go.

———————

Toe–Toe and Nard sat at the table in their mother's dining room, eating the meal she had cooked for her pride and joy. They were catching their mom up on everything that had been going on with Coach K. She had insisted that they come to her house after they left the hospital.

"Coach K should've slowed his old ass down and left all that mess to all of you, young folks. He got all that damn money; it's no reason for him to still be in these streets. He needs to retire. I bet if Beloved were still alive, he would have been left that shit alone. They probably would be living out the best years of their lives somewhere on a beach far from Atlanta." She remembered when they all were living in the fast lane.

"Momma, that is easier said than done. He has four kids still in these mean streets. Don't you know if Pops were still alive, he would be in the trenches with Nard and me? Real niggas do real shit. He is doing what he is supposed to do." Toe-Toe thought fondly about his and his brother's relationship with their dad. This street shit was definitely in their bloodline, but he was showing his son a different way, a better way.

Nard pushed his plate away and rubbed his belly. There was nothing like a home-cooked meal from Mom dukes. Her food was legendary on the Westside. His phone started to ring, and he picked it up but didn't recognize the number. "Yo," he answered, thinking it was a girl playing on the phone.

"Hey man, it's a black-on-black Phantom that just pulled up on top of the hill, " the person said on the other line.

Nard looked at Toe-Toe. "Hey man, didn't D.J. say last night that bitch Beautiful had bought a Phantom with Gorgeous money?" He looked at his brother with raised eyebrows as the wheels in his head started to turn.

"Yeah, I got some of my young goons looking for that bitch right now. She doesn't have anything on her head yet but trust me; I know that if we get her, a reward will definitely be granted." Toe-Toe said, letting his brother know that he was on the job.

"Well let's collect this bread, baby," he said to his brother as he spoke into the phone. "Get that bitch, man." He put the cell phone face down on the table and looked up.

"Who was that?" Toe-Toe scooted to the edge of his seat. He was always ready for everything.

"Dat was Rich. He believes Beautiful is sitting on the hill in front of her old apartment building. I told him to get her and bring her to us. Get Coach on the line."

"That girl got the balls of an elephant. I can't believe she had the nerve to enter our territory like everything was all good. She got to know how we rock with Coach them; that's family." Toe-Toe said to Nard as he stood up.

"Don't hurt that girl. I know she is half-crazy shit Solitaire was all the way crazy, and she still was my friend. Y'all don't know all that she has been through. Her mom was one of my good friends. Please don't hurt her. She has been hurt enough. Trust me, there is a method to her madness." Mom Dukes told her boys as they headed toward the front door.

"Momma, you don't get to worry 'bout us hurting her, but your boy Coach K is a whole nother story," Nard said as they walked out the door.

"Speak for yourself, nigga. I know that bitch is the reason why Killa was in that accident. I want that bitch's head. My young gunna ain't going never to be the same no more." Toe-Toe said through his teeth. He knew in his heart that Poke was just a puppet on Beautiful's string. She was the mastermind, and it was only a matter of time before everything came out."

Chapter Twenty-Two

I THINK I SAW A GHOST

Coach K had rushed home immediately after his reluctant release from the hospital. He didn't know which way to turn. He wanted to get in his truck and ride on some niggas. Ponchees insisted on coming over. He didn't stop him because he needed someone to talk to. He felt like he was going to explode. He looked at his watch, which the kids had gotten him for his last birthday, and tears fell. They had gone all out and got him the Audemars Piquet watch he had his eyes on. He had made these children his life. His every move was well thought out and acted upon because of his kids. But now, as his world seemed to be crumbling around him, he couldn't help but think that he had failed them.

He had called all the captains in the city and told them to be on the lookout for Beautiful, something that he should have done before things got this far out of hand. He had a private detective and Reality working on finding Honesty and locating Beautiful's last whereabouts. He didn't want to get the police involved, but the private detective was one of the best in the game. He was a retired FBI agent who occasionally did work for Coach K. His heart was telling him to call the official law enforcement, but his mind was telling him to keep them out of his business and that everything would be fine. He knew one thing: he wasn't leaving a stone unturned.

The doorbell rang, and it seemed to echo. This house was too big for just him alone. Despite the circumstances, he was happy that he had Loyalty and Killa here. He shook his head as he slowly got up from the barstool at the island and went to the door. He pulled his gun from his waistline as he unlocked the door and pulled it open. He blinked and then rubbed his eyes. There was a young lady in nurse scrubs at the door who bore an uncanny resemblance to Killah's girlfriend, Leigh.

"Please come in," he said just above a whisper. His voice was caught in his throat as he thought to himself that she might not be a good match.

"Good evening, sir. I hope it is not too late to come by and check on the patient. I just arrived back in town, and the doctor told me it was okay to stop by to introduce myself. I was supposed to be asking for someone named Loyalty." The young lady's voice was melodic.

"You are fine, my dear; I am her father. I think she is resting right now. Please come in. I'm Khalil Rasheed." He moved slowly and winced in pain.

"You look like you need someone to look after you as well. Please have a seat. Are you okay?" She looked at the handsome older gentleman with the tank top and dress slacks. She couldn't help but notice the gun in his hand. Instantly, she knew that his arm was in a sling because of a gunshot wound.

She ushered him into the den and helped him sit softly on the plush sofa. She propped his feet up and placed a large remote control at his side. When she looked over at him, he was smiling at her. "Is there anything else you need?"

"Yes, what is your name? Because I am about to start calling you Nurse Nightingale." Coach K said to the young lady. The more he looked at her, the more he thought about how much she resembled Leigh. He didn't know if this would be a good or bad thing for Killa, but he had already fallen in love with the young lady's spirit, just like he did the day he met Leigh. She might be just what the doctor ordered for his son.

"My name is Amor Jones," she said as she looked around the spacious den.

"Love Jones, that is a beautiful name. My wife's name was Beloved. I probably should have shown you to my son's room before you helped me settle down. I don't want to move now." Coach K had relaxed his body weight against the soft cushions and gotten comfortable for the first time since he got home.

"I don't want you to move. If you tell me where to go, I can go and check on your son and see if he needs anything. I know the doctor said he had taken him off all the sedatives because he wanted him to start trying to move around and get adjusted to tolerating whatever pain on his own." Amor felt slightly uncomfortable under the older gentleman's intense stare.

"He is in the suite right down the hall. Go back out like you are headed toward the foyer and make a right. It is the second door on the left. The door should be open, but still knock so you will not startle him." Coach K directed the young lady toward where his son was, and he wanted to get up and go with her because he wanted to see his son's reaction to the girl who looked so much like Leigh.

As Amor walked down the hall, anticipation took over her body. This was her first private duty case. Actually, he was her first patient since she had returned stateside from Afghanistan. She was so ready to return to life as a civilian. She had seen so much in her seven years in the military; she was ready to turn over a new leaf. This was her new beginning.

She tapped lightly on the door and peeked in. The bedroom was beautifully decorated and humongous—it seemed to be almost the size of her entire loft apartment. "Hello, are you awake?" Amor stepped inside the dimly lit room that smelled like lavender and vanilla.

When Killa heard the voice, he instantly looked over to the chaise lounge where his sister had made her second home since he had come home from the hospital. It was empty. Maybe he was dreaming that Leigh was standing in the doorway. But why did she have on hospital scrubs? He adjusted the hospital bed so that he would be in an upright position. "Leigh, I have been praying to Allah that you would return, and my prayers have been answered. What took you so long?"

Amor walked closer to the young man in the hospital bed. She looked around to see who he was talking to; she was the only person in the room. She knew that he had just come off heavy sedatives, so there was a chance that he was hallucinating. He was looking at her with the same intense stare his father had. They looked so much alike. She smiled on the inside as she thought he would be even more handsome in twenty years.

"Hello, Mr. Rasheed, my name is Amor. I will be your nurse. I hope that I didn't wake you. I'm sorry for coming so late, but I just got off a plane from Washington, DC. I need to check your vitals and see if you need anything." She reached for his chart on the nightstand and then took his temperature and blood pressure.

When the blood pressure cuff tightened around his bicep, Killa knew he was not dreaming. She looked so much like Leigh, but this wasn't her touch. He didn't know if he should be happy or if he should be sad. He felt a dull ache below his knee where the rest of his leg should be. Even before the doctor said that he was taking him off all the medication, he had his mind made up that he was not going to be in a drug-induced stupor all the time.

Killa watched as she wrote his blood pressure on the chart and placed it back. "How is my pressure?" His voice cracked. He was parched.

"It is slightly elevated, but there is nothing to be alarmed about. Once the medicine is out of your system, it should level out. Let me check your breathing. Please lean forward if you can." Amor watched him grunt and shift his weight forward as she put the stethoscope on his back and listened to his breathing.

"My sister has been helping me so much lately. She needs a break. Can you get me some juice or water, please? The refrigerator is right over there." Killa pointed to the other side of the room.

"No problem, that is what I'm here for. Is that all that you need? I know your sister is tired. Taking care of you and your father has to be a lot of work." Amor walked over to the small refrigerator. It was wood-grained and matched the furniture. She would never have known it was a refrigerator if he hadn't told her.

"Pop's gets around better than men half his age, and he is hardly here. She just has me acting like a big baby," Killa said as she reached out and grabbed the coconut water from Amor.

The doorbell rang loudly. "I will get that since your father said your sister is resting."

"Wayment, my father is home? He hasn't even come in to check on me." Killa frowned as he watched the girl who looked like Leigh walk out the bedroom door. He wished he could be more of a help to his father.

Leigh and Loyalty made it to the front door at the same time.

Loyalty did a double take when she looked at the young lady who grabbed the doorknob before she did. She looked just like Leigh. She wanted to cry. It had to be her hormones. It seemed like she could cry at the drop of a dime.

Ponchees stepped inside. "Good evening, ladies; where is your old man?" He said as he kissed Loyalty on the cheek.

"I'm not sure. I didn't even know that he was home." Loyalty said, staring at Leigh.

"Mr. Rasheed is resting in the den, sir," Amor said just above a whisper.

They all entered the den and found Coach K dozing off the sofa.

Loyalty immediately noticed her father's arm in the sling and the blood-soaked bandage on his shoulder. "Pop's, what happened to you." She rushed over to her father's side after startling him awake with her outburst.

Chapter Twenty-Three

CURIOSITY GOT DA CAT

Lil' Poke sat on Beautiful's sofa in the dark. The concierge had been busy playing a game on his phone or texting because she didn't even look up as Lil' Poke opened the door to the stairwell heading up toward the floor Beautiful lived on. The flimsy lock on her door gave way quickly to his credit card. He didn't even have to pick the lock. The only light illuminating her living room was the streetlights and the full moon in the sky.

He had come over for some answers and didn't plan to leave until he got them. Everybody's finger was pointed toward Beautiful for all the turmoil that was going on, even the death of his father. He couldn't believe she would do that.

The sex that he had with Beautiful the last time he showed up had him so thrown off that he didn't know if he was coming or going, but he wasn't going to let her get that far this time. Tonight, he had more than twenty questions, and he felt that Beautiful could answer them or point him in the right direction.

Boredom and curiosity got the best of him as he sat in the dark, waiting for her. He used this time alone to his advantage as he got up and looked around. The two-bedroom condo was very nicely decorated, with different hues of blue throughout. Lil' Poke walked into the main bedroom. The four-poster mahogany bed was unmade, clothes were on the floor, and her laptop was on the nightstand as if Beautiful was rushing when she left. He walked over to her dresser and opened a rhinestone-encrusted jewelry box sitting on top. Instead of the diamonds that he expected, it was filled with cocaine, three big rocks, and then a tiny mirror with a mound of off-white powder and a razor blade on it. He shook his head; he remembered all the stories that he had heard about her mother, Solitaire, and her drug abuse over the years. Beautiful was indeed her mother's daughter.

He walked over to a door he suspected was her closet and opened it. The closet was much larger than he thought. There weren't many clothes hanging on the hangers. Designer shoe boxes were stacked to the ceiling all across the shelves on both sides, bags from various stores littered the closet floor, and as he bent down and looked through them, he could tell that she had yet to wear most of them. These were not the clothes he was used to seeing her in. Beautiful always took extreme pride in her body and didn't hesitate to show it off. These clothes were not revealing and a lot classier, more like what her sister would wear. Then it hit him: Beautiful was pretending to be Gorgeous. But if that's the case, where was the real Gorgeous?

He needed to talk to Coach K. He exited the closet and closed the door behind him. The laptop on the nightstand caught his eye as he saw movement on the screen. He walked over to the side of the bed and picked it up. What he had seen on the screen almost made him drop it. He closed the laptop and rushed out of the condo at full speed to Coach K's house.

Chapter Twenty-Four

JUST HOLD ON, WE'RE GOING HOME

Although Honesty didn't want to leave Gigi alone, she knew it was their only hope. She couldn't just sit there and watch her die without trying to get some help. It seemed like her legs didn't want to move as fast as her mind wanted them to. She walked as steadily as possible to the exit and glanced over her shoulder at Gigi in the puddle of blood. Honesty silently prayed that someone would pass by who could help them when she walked outside.

She opened the heavy metal door slowly, and it seemed like it took all her strength. The cool night air hit her face, and she instantly shivered. Honesty was afraid to let the door close all the way because she didn't know if it would lock automatically once it closed. She kept one foot inside the door, put half her body out the door, and looked around on the ground for something strong enough to keep the door from closing. A brick was a few feet away, but she was scared that she wouldn't be able to move fast enough to get the brick and make it back to the door before it closed. As she leaped forward quickly, she heard all her bones creak as if she was an old woman. She grabbed the brick while her foot was still inside the door. She put the brick inside the door and let it close slightly.

The moon was full in the night sky as Honesty put her arms inside her shirtsleeves and ambled down Whitehall toward the closest traffic light. There wasn't a car in sight. She looked up at the sky to try to determine what time of the night it was. She reached the traffic light but still didn't see a car. Honesty crossed at the light and went to the lofts across the street. A car was coming out the gate, and she waved frantically at the driver. He didn't even stop. He blew his horn and proceeded down the street.

Tears started to fall from her eyes as she realized this was not going to be as easy as she thought it would be. Honesty thought that as soon as she walked out of the warehouse, she would be able to flag down help for them. It had to be the middle of the night because no one was around. After standing in front of the building for a few minutes, waiting for someone else to come out, she decided to walk back to the warehouse to make sure that Gigi was okay.

Gigi lay on her back with her eyes opened partially. Her breath was labored. She felt a breeze coming in, and with it, the smell of the warehouse intensified. She smelled her urine, her sweat, and her blood. Everything seemed so unreal to her. She wanted to live, but more people loved her in heaven than on earth. She couldn't believe that she was about to die from a bullet that was shot from her sister's gun. No matter how much they seemed to hate each other, she still loved her sister. Beautiful was just like their mother, and Gorgeous was just like their Aunt Brilliant, who constantly gave their mother chances.

"Why are you always so mean to Mommy? She loves us, Gigi. If you keep being mean to her, she will never come home. Try to be nice when she comes back to visit." Beautiful said as they lay in the bed together after their bath.

"You don't see her for what she is. A real mommy wouldn't visit us. She

would live with us. Solitaire needs to get her stuff together. She loves the streets more than she loves her children." Gigi said very matter-of-factly, sounding much older than her eight years.

"How can you say something like that? You are just repeating what you heard the grown folks saying." Beautiful said as she sucked on her bottom lip and played with her sister's long plait.

"I didn't hear anybody say anything about Solitaire. I have eyes; they just happened to be more open than yours because I see her for who she really is. All you see is the stars when she comes around. I bet Handsome sees the same thing I see. Just ask him." Gigi looked at the twin bed in the corner and saw their brother pull the cover over his head. She knew he hated being in the middle of their fights and debates.

She wondered if their mother had never made her appearances, would there even be any divide between her and her sister? She knew her mother didn't like her, and she always tried to make it seem like she was evil because she didn't want to be around her or acknowledge her as her mother. Gigi couldn't help but wonder how their lives would have played out without Solitaire.

The breeze coming through the door didn't help that she was already freezing. Gigi hoped her angels in heaven were with her because she wasn't ready to leave yet. Where was her earthly angel, Concrete, when she needed him? She inhaled and exhaled loudly despite the pain. "Please, God, help me, please."

"Was I so bad? You never loved me. I did the best that I could. You never gave me any credit at all. I was sick, Gorgeous, I didn't know how to be a mother, but I love all three of you. You all were the best thing that ever happened to me. I was always so proud of you. You did an outstanding job. You did something I couldn't do as a child as an adult. Please forgive me and know I loved you despite everything I said and did." Solitaire said.

Gigi closed her eyes tightly. She was praying to her angels in heaven, why did Solitaire appear? Maybe she was dying. She opened her eyes and saw that her mother was no longer there. She was so uncomfortable lying on the hard concrete floor. Her bones had started to ache from the hardness and the fact that she was lying so still. Why was it taking Honesty so long to come back with help?

"I forgave her. She is a part of me, just like you are a part of her. The doors to heaven wouldn't open so easily for me if I didn't make peace with her, among other people who had wronged me and who I had wronged. Don't let the fact that you are so stuck in your ways cause you to skate into hell on rollerblades. She is your mother, Gorgeous, and she was sick. Just believe with your heart that if your mother weren't suffering from Schizophrenia, she would have been a better mother to you and your siblings." Black Sillk said to Gorgeous.

"Can you please save me? I'm not ready yet." Gorgeous said to the first man to hold her heart.

"You can save yourself. Cleanse your heart, my child, and remember, no matter how much you think it, no one owes you anything." His voice echoed, and suddenly, Black Sillk was no longer standing before Gigi, looking like his usual healthy self.

"Do you think I kept score every time I did something for my sister? Do you think I added a notch to my belt every time I had to stay up late to open the door for her when she was in the streets? Do you think that I paid attention to how much money she borrowed from me and never gave me back? Do you think that I got on her over and over when I had to nurse her back to health after she had overdosed? Do you think I constantly threw it in her face that I was raising her kids while she was out having fun? Have you ever heard me do this to your mother? No, you didn't; God was keeping score; that is why I'm sitting on high with him right now.

"I was the smartest in my class in high school; I could've been anything I wanted to be. But no, I was happy staying home and caring for people. My momma would have died a lot sooner if I wasn't there to help her. Your mother would've died a lot sooner if I wasn't there to help her, and there is no telling

where you all would've been. We took all of you home from the hospital. Solitaire loved you all, but she didn't want you all and couldn't handle you all. I was fulfilling my mission, and while doing it, I wasn't counting the points I was scoring or making people feel bad about it. There is a saying that God always takes care of fools and babies. There is your answer, which is why your mother is in heaven with me. She is healthy in her mind, body, and spirit. Nobody is perfect. He forgave her, and you know what? I never gave up on my sister. Don't give up on yours. Y'all are even more special; you are identical." Brilliant stood up with her back straight, with no cane, walker, or crutches. In heaven, polio didn't exist.

"But Auntie Brilliant, she has killed people. She is evil." Gorgeous said to her aunt, who had raised her as if she was her own.

"Gorgeous, stop it right now! You have killed people." Brilliant vanished in a flash of light.

"Vengeance is mine, said the lord. Vengeance is mine, said the lord. Vengeance is mine, said the lord. We are not judge and jury. Tell me what will happen if you go to that club of yours and one of those dancers is on the computer ordering liquor. You would get mad because she is doing your job without asking. Trying to take matters into your own hands means taking things out of the Lord's hands. When that man was beating me, I still went to work. I still cleaned his house and cared for his kids; I still ironed his clothes and cooked his food. I was praying for a way out. I could've killed him in his sleep or went down to his job and got him fired. I didn't do that because I knew that my father in heaven had my back and he would make a way out of no way. In the end, Columbus suffered, and he was alone. God had my back and my front and both my sides. Let it go and let God have his way." She leaned over and touched Gorgeous' wound and kissed her forehead.

"Grandma, please tell me what to do!" Her voice was loud, and it didn't hurt as much when she hollered. Grandma Christine had disappeared into thin air just like everybody else. She knew that they said two things happen whenever you are about to die. One, you see dead people, and two, you get strength from out of nowhere. Gigi rolled from her back to her side and hardly felt any pain. She wanted to get up. She was sitting up in a puddle of blood with urine on her.

Honesty opened the heavy door, and in the middle of the floor, Gigi was sitting upright, looking at her. She rushed over to her. "Baby, what are you doing sitting up? How? I mean, when I left, you could hardly breathe." She felt the pulse on her neck, and it was strong, but she still had lost a lot of blood.

"I think my grandmother just healed me. She touched where the bullet went in." Gorgeous said to a wide-eyed Honesty, who was staring at her in bewilderment.

"Your grandmother?" She reached out and touched Gorgeous' head to see if she had a temperature.

"Yes, Christine, Brilliant, Solitaire, and Black Sillk were here." A smile spread across Gorgeous' face like she was not sitting in a pool of blood.

Chapter Twenty-Five

MISSING IN ACTION

Reality couldn't sleep. Her oldest sister had been kidnapped. She sat at the desk that D.J. had recently bought for her, with two screens going on her Mac. A migraine kicked in When D.J. came home after being out with her dad and told her everything that was going on as the wheels churned inside her head. It seemed as if she had existed in a love-induced coma because she couldn't believe all that was going on right under her nose, and she didn't see anything. This was so unlike Reality because she was the one out of all the sisters who were always suspicious of everything and anyone. She didn't have a sixth sense. She had a seventh sense, a gift in her line of business.

Honesty hadn't had any account activity on her credit cards, and the balance on her bank accounts was still the same. Reality had found the two offshore accounts that her sister had set up, which were still intact. As she went through her sister's phone records, she noticed that her sister had not used either of her cell phones. The last outgoing phone call was placed to a restaurant and had to be powered off because there hadn't been any incoming calls. It was like she fell off the face of the earth. If she was kidnapped, why hadn't a ransom been requested? But what if she wasn't kidnapped for money? And why hadn't Gigi said something about her disappearance to them? She acted like everything was okay.

She called her father and got the information needed to view the surveillance on their building and parking deck. Reality sat speechless as she watched a Chevy Malibu come through the gate, followed by a black Panamera and a black Yukon on its bumper. The two black vehicles almost wrecked, trying to enter the gate before it closed.

A guy left the Malibu with two bags in his hand and headed toward the building. He pushed the buzzer and was buzzed in. The female went right behind him when the door opened. The two of them got out on Honesty's floor, and then the surveillance showed him ringing the doorbell. Next, it showed her with a pistol hitting him in his head, stepping over his body, and going inside. Minutes passed, and then two men were buzzed in the building's entrance. They took the elevator to Honesty's floor as well. The screen went blank on her computer.

Reality hit the return key, but nothing happened. She tapped it several times before realizing they must have done something to the cameras. She leaped up from her desk, screaming throughout the condo, "Bae, come on! We must go to Pop's house. A.S.A.P."

D.J. came padding into the office and stood in the door. He was tired but had felt Reality tossing and turning, so he knew she wouldn't sleep anytime soon. "What's up, babe? You found something?"

Reality showed D.J. the footage. He didn't say anything when it was finished. He immediately left the room to go and change clothes. They had to get that to Coach K right away, without a doubt. Too much time had passed already. He had been praying for them. When he went and saw the Chief to offer prayer for them, he saw bloodshed, but they were still alive. D.J. was still optimistic because the Chief never led him wrong.

They were on the highway headed north, riding in silence. But both of them were deep in thought about the situation at hand. D.J. wondered why in the hell this family had been targeted, and Reality wondered how far Beautiful would go.

With one arm in a sling and walking slower than usual, Coach K was headed out the front door of the house to his truck when Reality and D.J. pulled up.

"Pop's, where are you going at this time of night? We got something to show you." Reality asked her father as Ponchees came out the door behind him.

"He is going to get himself killed. Talk some sense into him. I think all that medicine they gave him when he got shot has taken control of his brain." Ponchees said to Reality.

"You know how many niggas I've put in the ground? No, wait, don't answer that. It takes two hands to kill nobody, as long as my trigger finger works. I kill better than I do anything else. I don't need any help. I'm going to dead everything walking until I get answers about where my daughter and Gorgeous are." Coach K was dressed in all black with a black skullcap covering his bald head. He had learned his lesson last time; this time, he wore a lightweight body armor suit.

Reality looked at D.J., hoping he was about to say something to discourage her father from whatever he was about to do. He turned around, pushed the seat forward in his truck, and pulled an AR 15 from a hidden compartment behind his seat. He then removed the door speaker and took out two chrome nine-millimeter pistols. He put all the firepower on the seat, opened the toolbox on the back of his truck, and got out a bulletproof vest and double shoulder holster.

"You ain't leaving without me. I got your back," D.J. said as he walked around to get in the passenger seat of Coach K's truck. He didn't know his plan or where he was going; he just knew that he wouldn't let his future father-in-law go to war by himself.

"Aye, yi, yi? Can we at least take my truck? Is it bulletproof?" Ponchees said to them as he walked down the steps and headed toward his truck, where his driver had been inside all this time reading car and bike magazines.

The three men got into Ponchees' truck with a lot of ammunition. Coach K was prepared. He was going to the apartments that Miami Black had told him about.

"So what is the plan?" D.J. asked Coach K as he put his two pistols in the holsters.

Chapter Twenty-Six
BEAUTIFUL DISASTER

Beautiful glanced up, and a face was at the car window with his hands cupped, trying to peer inside the dark tint. Panic filled her because she didn't know if she had been discovered. She had done so much over the past few months; she was living on eggshells.

"You good, Miss Lady?" Rich said to Beautiful. He could see the fear in her eyes but didn't see the recognition. He was going to try to play this off as just being concerned. She was looking at him behind the tint, blinking the most beautiful eyes he had ever seen. Damn, no wonder her name was Beautiful. She looked just like her sister, but there was something different that he couldn't quite put his finger on.

Beautiful looked straight ahead, not knowing that his green eyes could see every move she made. She reached over to Hermes's bag in the passenger seat for her pistol as her hand shook nervously. In a split second, glass shattered as the man took the butt of a chrome pistol and busted the driver-side window.

His first instinct told him to shoot the window out as he saw her reach over toward her pistol. He had heard all of the accusations. Rich knew that Beautiful was deadly and would not let her looks throw him off. He was told to bring her back alive, which he planned to do. He hit the window once with the butt of his chrome nine-millimeter pistol. Beautiful looked up, and her eyes seemed to pierce his soul. They stared at each other.

All she needed was that moment of hesitation from him. As she stared at him, her eyes darted to stare down the barrel of the pistol that he had pointed directly between her eyes. Beautiful put the car in reverse and punched the gas. She knew she had rolled over his feet or hurt him even worse. She ducked low as the bullets ripped through the quarter of a million-dollar vehicle. The Phantom was everything but bulletproof. The back window shattered, and a bullet tore through the seat. She felt the heat as the bullet entered her side. Her eyes rolled in the back of her head as she pictured how she had left her sister on the ground, bleeding to death in the abandoned warehouse. They had come into the world at the same time, the same way, and they were dying the same way. Payback is a motherfucker.

"They say that you are like me. You are nothing like me! I fought until I took my last breath. Your punk ass sitting here about to give up on the life you have been wanting. Well, die bitch, but just know you've taken enough lives to know you ain't going to heaven to chill out." Solitaire said from the passenger seat. The cigarette was dangling in her mouth as she talked to her daughter.

Beautiful looked up, and she was on Hollywood Road. She had passed out. The gunfire had stopped, and she didn't see her assailant. This was the Westside; there was no way possible that she would be able to make it from here without getting either locked up or killed. She needed help. Beautiful rubbed her eyes; Solitaire was gone, and her voice was mocking her. She tried to think of whom she could call.

She pulled over in the first abandoned house she saw when she turned off on Church Street. Now was the time she needed someone. The tears flowed freely from her eyes, not because of the pain ripping through her side but because she had no one. She had shitted on everyone who had ever helped her. She didn't want to call her brother; only two other people would help her without asking questions. Beautiful grabbed her cell phone and called May-May. His phone went to voicemail immediately. What in the hell was she paying him for if he wasn't on standby, she wondered. She then dialed a number she had not called in two years.

"Tristan Ball, how can I help you?" The deep voice said on the other end. He heard the heavy breathing and repeated himself. When he didn't get a response, he hung up, but he stared at the phone as a weird feeling came over him, which prompted him to redial the unfamiliar number.

Beautiful could barely hold her eyes open. She was feeling so tired. The ringing of the phone startled her. It was Tristan calling her back. "Please, I need you, Tristan. I'm sorry. Help me, I'm dying."

"Who is this?" Tristan heard the labored breathing on the other end of the phone. He tried to recognize the voice. He thought he had left that life behind in Haiti.

"I've been shot. I'm so alone. Please save me, Tristan." Beautiful uttered just above a whisper. It seemed like even breathing was making her tired.

Fear filled him, and his thoughts of his old life returned as he repeated. "Who is this?"

"This is Beautiful, please come help me."

Tristan jumped up in the bed when he heard her name. "Where are you? Where do I need to come to? I'm on my way." He had been looking for her for what seemed like forever.

"I'm on the Westside on Church Street. It's a side street off Perry Boulevard and Hollywood Road."

"I'm at my condo. I can be there in less than fifteen minutes. You are injured and need medical attention. I'm about to call an ambulance because I'm afraid you might not make it." He was nervous. He would do anything to help her, but he didn't want to lose her in the process.

Through clenched teeth, Beautiful said, "Nigga, I could've called a muthafucking ambulance. I want you to come help me. I need you, not a paramedic. So get here now!"

And just like a puppet on the string, one of the most powerful men in the music industry jumped at her command and ran to her rescue.

———————

Tristan silently prayed for Beautiful as he exited the parking garage at his condo in the Twelve. It was meant for him to be staying in town instead of at his estate in Eagles Landing. He had put many things behind him when he came to America and changed his identity, but now he was going to have to use some of the resources that he had used when he was the head of the Haitian Mob. Tristan hardly called his brother and had not seen him since he was released from the federal prison for wire fraud. He had closed that chapter of his life but didn't know who else to turn to for help in this area. He called Brian.

"Aye, it's me. I need you to put me on with a doctor who sees patients at their homes. I'm on the Westside of Atlanta. I'm not sure how badly she is injured, but she has been shot and time is of the essence."

Tristan was turning from Marietta Street to Perry Boulevard before he knew it. He didn't realize he was driving so fast, but he was happy no police were in the area.

"Her, man, it's a bitch? Take her to the hospital. You ain't a gangster anymore. You have no reason to hide. Everything is good now, big brother. You will seem like the hero. Big record executive rescues the damsel in distress and brings her to the hospital." Brian had not seen his brother since he dropped him off at the apartment he had gotten for him when he was released from prison, and now he was calling him asking him for advice.

"Don't fucking play with me, B. Call your people, 'cause I know you got people, and tell them you got a gunshot victim that needs to be seen A.S.A.P. What's their address?"

Brian could hear the seriousness in his brother's voice, so he did as he was told. Chancellor had always been a fool for a bitch. That was the main reason he had moved to Atlanta. Chasing a bitch almost got him with a murder charge in Miami. "He owes me a favor; I will call him and give him the logistics, then I will send you the address. Oh, and Chance, be mindful. Remember what happened the last time you got wrapped up in a bitch."

"Preciate it, lil' bro and my name is Tristan. Chance is dead," he said as he turned on Church Street and let the window down to look for Beautiful. The streetlights were out, there was overgrown grass, and old tires dumped everywhere. He slowed down as he approached the first house, and he saw the black Phantom filled with bullet holes in the driveway, still running.

"Baby, so you just gonna give up like that? I thought you had so much to live for. What happened to you opening up the home for abused girls? What happened to you writing books? Those were your dreams. You haven't accomplished anything, and you obviously won't if you are giving up on life so easily." Jamal's voice said to Beautiful from the passenger seat.

"I can't do that by myself. You should have never left me. Why did you leave me, Jamal? I had nobody left but you. If I die, then I will be with you again. You don't want me?" Beautiful wept for the pain that she felt physically and for the pain she felt mentally. She didn't have a reason to live. Nobody loved her, and nobody wanted her. She closed her eyes, and her breathing became even shallower.

Tristan sprinted to the car and pulled on the door handle. It was locked, and Beautiful slumped over into the passenger seat. Her entire side was filled with blood. He reached into the shattered window and opened the door. She was unconscious, so he reached for her neck to check for her pulse. It was faint. "Beautiful, don't die on me, you hear me? I've been waiting for you all my life. I need you. I'm about to get you some help."

Beautiful moaned as Tristan picked her up. "Jamal, I want to come be with you in heaven. Ask God to let me in heaven. I won't be bad anymore."

Tristan didn't say anything as he heaved her limp body into his arms and carried her the short distance to his Mercedes G wagon. He opened the back door, gently placed her body in, and shut the door silently. He moved the pistol out of his seat and got in. His brother texted the address to his phone. He copied and pasted the address into his Google Maps app on his iPhone and headed up Perry Blvd towards the West Paces Ferry address.

Chapter Twenty-Seven

SWEET SADIE

K.J. didn't give the driver time to open his door. He jumped out of the blacked-out Escalade as soon as it pulled up in front of his grandmother's house. He looked around at the beautiful grounds of the estate he had purchased for his grandmother as soon as he signed his NFL contract. He was surprised his grandmother wasn't outside tending to all her flowers or picking something from her garden. Although she had a gardener to tend to the acres of land, she still liked getting her hands dirty daily in the soil.

He had left his crutches and boot at home; he only had the Aircast on his foot. His grandmother must have seen the car out of the window. She opened the door, stood on the porch, and watched him as he limped up the cobblestone walkway with the chauffeur behind him carrying a duffle bag and a briefcase. To see his grandmother smiling so happily because he was home made him smile. Coming home was just what he needed.

"Kay, now you put me down right now. I know I don't weigh but a hundred pounds soaking wet, but you might hurt yourself. You came home to get well, not to hurt yourself some more." Sadie Weaver beamed with pride at her grandson.

"Big Mama, you know I can lift six or seven of you simultaneously. I'm not going to hurt myself. Wrap your arms around me and hug me. You act like you are not happy to see your boy." K.J. put his grandmother down softly on the porch and reached into his pocket to tip the driver after placing his bags in the foyer.

"Oh my goodness, God bless you, sir. God Bless you, " the driver said enthusiastically as he looked down at the five crispy brand-new one-hundred-dollar bills the young man had just given him. He turned around and literally skipped back to the SUV.

"You get that from your daddy. When he started practicing his religion, I would see him give every homeless person he encountered on the street some money. He would do that even when he didn't have money to give. God bless his soul." Sadie strolled into the house.

"Why are you walking so slow? Is everything okay with you?" K.J.'s voice filled with worry. She had just had a hip replacement a few months ago, and she was up and around like she never had fallen and broke her hip to begin with.

"Boy, gone. I'm walking slowly so you can keep up with me. Aren't you the one with the hurt ankle? It sure doesn't look hurt to me. Where ya crutches?" Right then, as he walked beside her, she knew that the only thing hurting her grandson was his heart.

She entered the kitchen as K.J. walked into the formal living room and looked around. It seemed like he hadn't been home in forever. During his last trip, he only stopped by briefly; he had stayed at his condo downtown. Before then, it was when his grandmother was in the hospital for her surgery. K.J. sat down at the black baby grand piano and started playing a tune.

"That is the first thing you do every time you walk in that door. You act like you don't have one at home." She wiped her hands on her apron before sitting beside her grandson on the piano bench.

"Tell you the truth, Big Mama; I don't play it 'cause it doesn't feel the same unless you sit beside me. I think I only played it twice. Once when I first got it and once when Loyalty came to visit." K.J. changed the melody to the song he was playing and looked over at his grandmother, who was smiling from ear to ear.

"*Sweet Sadie, don't you know I love you, Sweet Sadie? Place no one above you, Sweet Sadie.*" K.J. never claimed to be a singer, but he could harmonize.

"Music is therapeutic. If just listening to it can make you feel good, imagine how good you would feel if you played it all the time. I know it sure is relaxing for me. Some nights, I come down here and bang on the keys like I have the whole church choir behind me. Those nights, I sleep like a baby and wake up fully rested."

"Why didn't you teach me piano? You have been playing so long?" K.J. had never asked his grandmother that. She had been playing the piano for the church for almost fifty years.

"I probably would have if I didn't have the money. I know how important music is. Your father's trust was established so you could have the best of the best. So, I figured you might as well be classically trained. I wanted you to be able to do many things professionally."

Sadie thought about her son and how he had doted on his children. She was happy that she was able to raise them both to be different from their father. She was also happy that her son's best friend had gotten his life together after his passing and helped her financially all these years. It could've been because of his guilty conscience that he was paving the road to redemption by taking on Khadafi's family. She told him almost twenty years ago that she and God forgave him, too.

She knew that the death took a toll on him even though he didn't pull the trigger. Her son's best friend had felt that he was responsible for his death.

The aroma drifted from the kitchen and hit his nose as soon as he stood up. He looked over at her and smiled. This lady really was his whole world. "I'm going to take a quick nap. By the time I wake up, whatever you are whipping up in there should be finished." K.J. grabbed his bags and proceeded through the living room toward the double staircase that led to the second floor. He stopped at the fireplace as he always did when he walked through and picked up one of the numerous pictures of his father throughout the house. This one was of his father and his father's best friend, whom he had never met. His eyes literally bucked in his head. The guy who stood with his arm wrapped around his father was Khalil Rasheed. He still looked almost the same. The only difference between now and then was the Taqiyah worn on his head.

K.J. snatched the picture off the mantle and sprinted into the kitchen like his ankle was never sprung. He burst through the swinging door, startling his grandmother as she stirred a large pot on the stove. "Who is this man?" his voice boomed.

His grandmother walked over to him and looked up at him with one eyebrow raised as she rubbed her hands on the front of her apron before taking the picture frame out of his hands. "Boy, who are you raising your voice at? You know who that is!" She handed him back the picture frame and prepared to go back to the stove.

"I know that it is his best friend. But what is his name, and why hasn't he come around in all these years? I know if one of my best friends were murdered, I would still be there for the children. This nigga fake!" Rage filled K.J. as he thought about how Loyalty's father had said that he had watched him over the years and knew about his career.

"How do you know that he hasn't been there? Calm down, don't go assuming." Sadie knew that it would be better if she told the story before her grandson started fishing and got the story misconstrued. She was heartbroken and mad at Coach K, but his dedication to her grandkids had softened her heart over the years. He called and checked on her three times a week and came to see her at least once a month. He was at every graduation ceremony the kids have had throughout their childhood. He was a good man. He had redeemed himself.

"Come on, Big Mama quit beating around the bush. I asked his name." K.J. tried to lower his voice. He didn't want his grandmother to think that he was disrespecting her. He just needed confirmation that this was indeed Coach K.

"His name is Khalil Rasheed. He was the one who found your father when he was murdered, and he was also the last person to see him alive. Baby, he has always been there in the shadows. Your father was in these streets hustling from meal to meal. I had life insurance on him, but it was only enough for his funeral service and burial. I wasn't expecting to be burying my twenty-five-year-old son. Coach K is the trust. He has been taking care of you and your sister all these years. He made sure that you guys had the best of everything. He also helped me fill in the gaps around here.

K.J. stood there with tears in his eyes. This was the first time his grandmother had ever even said the word murdered. She used always to say, "When your father was taken away from us." He tried to wrack his brain to think if he had seen Coach K over the years, and he couldn't recall. "If he had done so much good for us, why is he hiding in the shadows then, Big Mama? He has four kids of his own that he takes care of. The fact that he took on two that were not his kids is nothing to run from or be ashamed of. He should be commended. That is unless it's something that he isn't telling us. I gotta feeling it's something in the milk not clean, and I'm going to find out." K. J. turned to walk out of the kitchen.

"Son, just let sleeping dogs lie. I know all that I need to know. He didn't pull the trigger on the gun to kill your father. Whatever sins he committed against your father that I don't know about have been redeemed a hundredfold. Just let it be. Please!" Sadie pleaded with her stubborn grandson.

"I can't, Big Mama, I just can't," he shouted as he looked over his shoulder before he walked out of the kitchen.

"Why? Please, I beg of you. We might find out some things that are not any of our business. If you seek, you shall find." She knew she would have to call Coach K as soon as her grandson was out of earshot. And it was then that she thought about what he had just said about Coach K's four children. How did he know that? He was hiding something from her.

"I can't, Big Mama, because Loyalty is Coach K's daughter, and she is his spitting image." He stomped out of the kitchen, leaving the door swinging back and forth.

Chapter Twenty-Eight
STILL LIVING

It seemed like time was standing still as Lil' Poke pushed the Audi R8 to the floor on the highway heading to Coach K's house. The sun was about to peek through the clouds, and it would soon be daylight. He was thankful it was the weekend; otherwise, he would be trapped in wall-to-wall traffic. The adrenaline pumped through his veins. He knew this was the key to bringing Gorgeous and Honesty home.

Lil' Poke pulled up to the circular driveway behind some unfamiliar cars and hopped out with the laptop in his hand. He sprinted up the few stairs and started ringing the doorbell and simultaneously pounding on the front door. Somebody had to be awake. Lil' Poke knew that Coach K knew many people from everywhere, and he probably had everybody on this by now because he knew people high and low. As he stood waiting for someone to come to the door, he thought about what would happen to Beautiful. He knew they were going to order her to be murdered; she obviously had gotten away with so much. She had to suffer the consequences of her actions. He took a deep sigh when the door was finally opened, not because he was tired of knocking but because he had just realized that there was no way he could save her from them.

Reality's boyfriend, D.J., came to the door. "What's up, my G? I see the fire has been lit under everybody's ass. It seems like it just hit everybody that this is really happening, that Honesty and Gigi are actually missing."

Lil' Poke followed him into the den. Reality was sitting Indian-style on the floor with her MacBook Air open. Coach K, Handsome, and Ponchees sat huddled deep in conversation.

Handsome looked up from the conversation and smiled at Lil' Poke. "I've been calling you all night. Where you have been, man?"

"My phone must've died, but I was getting this!" He exclaimed as he held up the thin laptop computer in his hand.

Lil' Poke walked over to the cocktail ottoman and opened the computer. On the screen, Gorgeous and Honesty were tied up to two old wooden chairs back to back.

"Son, where did you get this? Is this live footage?" Coach K grimaced in pain as he leaned forward to get a better look at the screen.

"What is it? What's on the computer?" Reality rushed over to see what everyone was looking at. She picked up the computer, and it cut off.

D.J.'s eyebrow went up as he looked on. "What did you just do?"

"Oh shit! I wasn't even thinking about getting the charger. I had to get out of there quick, fast and in a hurry. Time is of the essence. Our first priority is getting the girls home safe and sound. We got to see what's on this computer. Ugh! Where in the hell are we going to get a charger?" Lil' Poke stood up and ran his hand through his hair in frustration.

Reality examined the computer. "Pop's, where is your adapter for your computer? The same company makes them, and it should fit."

Coach K leaned forward and prepared to get off the sofa. He grimaced in pain as D.J. rushed over to help him up. "I will go and get it."

"No sir, you need to rest. Tell one of us where it is. We can get it for you." D.J. said as he looked at Reality's father. The stress of everything was written all over his face. His cheeks looked hollow, and dark circles started to form around his eyes.

"I got it. Sit down somewhere, old man." Reality rushed past everyone and headed toward her father's office. She saw the nurse enter her brother's room and close the door. That reminded her that she needed to check on him while she was there.

When she returned, she handed the adapter to Lil' Poke as she listened to her father finally tell what happened when they left with all the guns.

"I had some intel on who worked for Beautiful and where they hung out. I rode through the neighborhood to check things out when I got the information that day. I didn't see anything out of the ordinary or the nigga I was looking for. I felt like tonight was the night, so I went over there. It was unexpected because they expected me to be in the hospital, recuperating or dead. From what you said earlier about the surveillance footage, the same niggas that shot me at the funeral were the same niggas that helped kidnap Gorgeous and Honesty" Coach K was running off pure adrenaline. He didn't feel the pain in his shoulder anymore.

"So, did you get anybody? What did you come up with tonight?" Lil' Poke inquired. He was worried about Beautiful, but he knew that he shouldn't be because she had turned into a monster, and he was not even going to be able to help her.

"Nobody was outside, and it was quiet, but the black Panamera and the Black Yukon were both parked right there, and I ripped them bitches to shreds with my A-R. So I hope them muthafuckers got other means of transportation." Coach K said before he got up from the couch and stretched.

"So I take it you know who works for Beautiful on this." Lil' Poke inquired.

"She always manages to get bottom feeders on her team. It's a nigga name May-May; he keeps a lot of young niggas up under him all the time. I can't say if they are in on this with him, but he is the prime suspect." Coach K said aloud before he could think.

Lil' Poke thought about what Coach K had said and walked swiftly out of the room. He was tired of lashing out at people in his father's defense. Poke was dead and gone. It was best to let sleeping dogs lie where they die. He headed in the direction of Killa's room. He had yet to see him since he was up and coherent.

Chapter Twenty-Nine

NO SUCH THING AS TOO LATE

Beautiful opened her eyes and closed them again swiftly. The sun was blinding her. She tried to inhale, but it hurt even to breathe. She tried to lift her hand to shield her eyes from the light but couldn't move. She had no idea where she was. She attempted to open her mouth to call for help, but she couldn't because she had a tube in her nose and it was taped to her mouth. She tried to lift her arm again, but everything was so heavy. She just opened and closed her hand repeatedly. There was nothing else she could do, and no other body part she could move. She prayed somebody would come into the room soon.

Tristan paced back and forth up and down the hall as he listened to his mother berating him over the phone. His brother had told his mother what he was doing. His mother and brother were the only people from his former life in Haiti who knew he was alive. He listened to everything she said, side-eyeing his brother simultaneously as he sat on the sofa in his living room.

Beautiful had been unconscious for almost a week. His brother was telling him to take her and leave her in front of the emergency room so she could get the care she needed. His mother agreed. He couldn't do that. He didn't know what Beautiful was involved in, but the last thing she said was, 'Don't take me to the hospital.' He was doing exactly what she told him to do. Tristan had the doctor that his brother recommended do what he could. He told him he was doing all he could; they just had to wait and see what would happen. He had a nurse coming over each afternoon to change her IV, clean her up, and check her vitals. The doctor came by every morning before he went to his job at the hospital. Tristan had ordered everything the doctor told him was needed for her care, but he was tired of waiting and praying.

"Please talk some sense into him, mama." Brian hollered so his mother could hear him. He was worried about his brother. He had to keep constantly telling him that he was treading shallow waters. He shouldn't be getting involved in all that shit. He had a new identity and career; he had gotten away scot-free. Opportunities like this did not come by, but once in a lifetime, it seemed as if his brother was about to blow it all over a woman. His brother was always a sucker for love. Brian had learned the hard way that everything was not foolproof. He had spent forty-eight months behind bars, and he definitely wasn't trying to get in trouble.

Tristan ended the call with his mother and turned to his brother. "Man, why did you have to go and call her? Now she is talking about getting on a flight and coming here. I got this under control. Please let me handle this." He had already been out of the office for a week. He was working from home. He told his staff that he was sick. He was bombarded with cards, balloons, flowers, and fruit baskets from his staff and those he worked with in the industry.

"We will not talk about the last time I let you handle something. I will help you take her to the truck. We will drop her off at the hospital and keep it moving. You can wait a day or two after she has been identified and then visit her. It is as simple as that." Brian planned to get his brother out of this; he just had to get him to go along with it.

"I'm not dropping anybody off at the hospital, and that is final. You can leave now. The nurse is coming in to clean her up, and I have an important conference call in ten minutes." Tristan was headed to check on Beautiful when the doorbell chimed.

"I will get it," Brian said as he got up from the sofa. He shook his head. He didn't know what it would take for his brother to come to his senses. He looked through the peephole, and it was a young lady standing there in a nurse's uniform. He opened the door, and she came in.

"Hello, I'm Nurse Jones. I am a little early; I hope it is not an inconvenience. I have another patient on the north side of town that I have to get to. It is better to be early than late."

"I apologize for staring. Please come in." Brian moved out of the doorway and allowed her to enter. She was beautiful but in a natural way. He noticed that she walked with a slight limp. He wondered what her story was. He knew his brother told him to leave, but he decided to stay until after his brother finished his call.

Looking around for the man of the house, Amor headed into the room with the patient. She didn't ask many questions. She had been blessed with two assignments that paid her well since coming back stateside. Neither of them spared any expense when it came to the care of their loved ones. She knew in her mind that she was getting paid not only for her skills as a nurse but also for her discretion. She saw things, but she acted like she didn't.

Amor noticed the patient's eyelids fluttering back and forth despite her eyes being closed. She probably was having a dream. This was the first time she had seen any type of activity. The young lady had been unconscious since she had been coming. Amor rushed to her side and pulled out her stethoscope to listen to her vital signs. The patient's eyes opened suddenly. It startled Amor because she hadn't expected it. Even more startling was the gray color of her patient's eyes. She listened to her vitals, and they seemed to be strong. She checked her

I.V. drip and made sure that everything was okay with her N.G. tube and her catheter. She needed to let the doctor and Mr. Ball know that the patient had awakened.

She turned to leave and felt a tug on her shirt. Amor turned around and the young lady had grabbed ahold of her. Her eyes were pleading to her not to go. She knew exactly what she was saying because she had been in the same situation.

Brian was walking toward his brother's office when he saw the nurse coming up the hall toward his office. "Is everything okay, nurse? I'm sorry that I was so rude earlier. Hello, my name is Brian, I am Tristan's younger brother."

"I figured as much, I could see the resemblance. I wanted to let Mr. Ball know that the patient was awake. I'm about to call the doctor right now." Amor walked around Brian and into Tristan's home office.

He held up one finger and signaled to tell her he was on a phone call. She stepped back out into the hallway and called the doctor. He told her he would be over within the hour and that if she had to leave to go to her next patient, she would ensure the young lady was clean and comfortable. He also told her to tell the patient not to pull on any of her tubing or IV.

She went back into the room and checked on her patient. There was something about the brother that creeped her out. She couldn't put her hand on it, but she hated how he watched her. Amor was excited that her patient had awakened, and she was even more excited that her other patient had received his prosthesis yesterday, so today, they were going to start therapy. She was anxious to help him start walking again.

Amor grabbed her hand and rubbed it. She remembered what it felt like to wake up and no one was there with you. Tears fell from the young lady's eyes. She reached into her scrub pocket, got a Kleenex, and wiped away her tears. She hated to leave her like this.

Mr. Ball walked into the room. Tristan's brother had told him the nurse said she was awake, and he couldn't get down the hall fast enough. He came in and went on the other side of the Tempur-Ergo bed that he had delivered on her second day in his home. It didn't matter what any of her treatment cost. He wanted her better. He reached for her hand, and he noticed the bruising from them sticking her so many times to find a vein for the IV.

He rubbed that area, bent his head down, and kissed that spot. "I'm so happy to see them beautiful eyes looking at me again."

Amor let go of her hand, entered the adjacent bathroom, and got the things she needed to start cleaning up the patient. She also wanted to allow Mr. Ball some time alone with his wife. The young lady had been shot, but Amor didn't recall hearing anything about it. With him being a prominent music executive, she thought that the incident would be everywhere in the media. It was obvious that it was some type of cover up, but money paid for everything, including quality hospital care in the privacy of your home. Amor just prayed that Mr. Ball wasn't the one who had shot the young lady. She got the small tub of warm water, the oatmeal soap, and washcloths, then returned and put everything on the nightstand next to the bed.

"Do you need any help with anything? I'm so happy that she is woke that I don't want to leave her side." Tristan was curious about what actually happened that night when he rescued her. He wondered who had done this to her and who Jamal was.

"Nope, I think I got it. I want to stay until the doctor comes, but I can't. He will call and brief me on everything, and let me know if he needs me to come back by after I'm done with my other patient. Also, you have my number in case anything arises."

Amor washed Beautiful's face, taking extra care and time around her eyes, getting all the dried tears and mucus from that had built up from being closed for a week. She removed the tape around her tubing, cleaned the area, and applied more tape before giving her a sponge bath. Mr. Ball volunteered to rub her down with the oatmeal lotion after she finished washing her.

The young lady's eyes were moving back and forth between them as they had their hands on her. She noticed that she grimaced when Amor was finished with her sponge bath. "Are you in pain? If you are, blink your eyes twice."

She rapidly blinked her eyes twice.

"Can you give her something to make her more comfortable? I don't want her in pain." Tristan said to the nurse.

"I can, but I won't. The doctor is on his way. I want her to be coherent enough to answer all of his questions and not to be under the influence of any medication. I'm heading out now, but I'm only a call away. I will see you tomorrow if I don't see you later tonight. Congratulations, I'm happy that your wife is awake." After putting up all the cleaning supplies, Amor packed her medical bag and headed to her next patient.

Brian was standing in the doorway, watching everything. His brother seemed to be really in love with the girl. He didn't know if he was mad at his brother for always finding love or if he was mad at him for always being a fool. He never corrected the nurse when she referred to the girl as his wife.

Chapter Thirty

SLEEPLESS IN ATLANTA

Gorgeous tossed and turned in her sleep. Honesty watched her, but she didn't disturb her. She sat in the chair across the room with the iPad in her lap, catching up on her reading. She had just finished reading "Resurrecting Midnight" by Eric Jerome Dickey. Now, she was reading the Atlanta Journal-Constitution to catch up on all the madness in her city. She was doing anything to keep from going to sleep. So much had happened to her, she was scared that if she closed her eyes, she would relive it. That seemed to be what Gigi was doing. Their days in the warehouse were numbered. Honesty was sure that if her father had not arrived when he did, they would've been dead sooner than later.

"Leave Honesty alone." Gigi opened her eyes wide and looked around, panicked. She then noticed where she was and started to calm down. Gigi was in Honesty's bedroom at her father's house. She exhaled loudly and felt the pain from her gunshot wound. She moaned in pain. "This lets me know that this was not a nightmare." She lifted her shirt and pointed to the bandaged spot where the bullet entered.

"I'm scared to go to sleep. The monster haunts me every time I close my eyes. I see Beautiful even when I close my eyes briefly." Honesty said to Gorgeous.

"Come here, get in the bed with me." Gigi pulled the covers back and gestured for Honesty to join her.

Honesty got in the bed with Gigi just as someone knocked on the bedroom door. "Come in."

Handsome walked into the bedroom. He looked exhausted. He sat down on the foot of the bed. He was so happy to see at least one of his sisters in one piece. "I'm not interrupting anything, am I?"

"No, I just woke up, and I'm trying to get my big baby a little rest. She will read every book released since we have been gone. I'm beginning to think that she has been taking something to stay awake because she acts like she isn't sleepy." Gorgeous said as she wrapped her arm around Honesty and pulled her close to her in the bed.

"This is probably what is keeping her awake." Handsome picked up an empty Red Bull energy drink can from the nightstand.

"Yup, that would do it. Give me this iPad, and let me see what books you have downloaded. Does Kwan have anything new yet? It seems like I have been waiting forever for his newest book to drop." Gigi took the iPad from Honesty's hand and looked at her book collection on her Kindle app.

"Yes, he got some novellas he recently released. I just downloaded them. But I can't wait for that either." Honesty said.

"Handsome, I need to go and see Concrete as soon as the sun comes up. I have been away from him too long. I feel like my rib is missing." Gigi had been missing Concrete something awful. Not a day passed that she wasn't worried about him. She knew if he were one hundred percent, that she and Honesty would never have been kidnapped.

"Speaking of missing, what will we do about our sister? Call the dogs off. They are hunting her to kill her. Talk to your men, Gigi. I'm praying that she is not dead; she has already been involved in a shootout." Handsome hoped that what he was saying would get through to his sister. She was stubborn and believed in issuing the death sentence to anyone who was not loyal, and right now, that person was Beautiful.

"Look Handsome, you see this right here? Bea's men did not cause this injury; she caused it. She shot me with her gun. Killa is downstairs learning how to walk with a fake leg. A little boy no longer has his mother, and another family has lost a daughter. Lil' Poke lost his dad, and Coach K got a hole in his damn shoulder. Concrete might not walk again, and you are asking me to spare this bitch? Come on man, you can't be serious. I just hope you got a nice insurance policy on her punk ass. God knows I do." Gigi lifted her shirt and showed her bandage that covered her bullet wound.

Handsome looked at Honesty for help, but she had dosed off in his sister's arms. "There has to be another way. Not only is this your sister, our sister. You are identical. Please, don't do it for her, do it for me, Gigi. Please do it for me." He pleaded with his sister. He knew that she had a heart.

"Okay, look. If I back off of Bea, that is just me. I'm not the only one she hurt. That bitch fucked over a lot of people, people who I don't have control over. You have known Killa and Lil' Poke all their lives. They are like our little brothers. Do you think they will let her go on about her merry way? She killed Killa's fiancé and Lil' Poke's dad. You know those boys' history. Or Do I need to get Uncle K up here to remind you?" Gorgeous knew she was powerful, but she also knew she didn't have enough power to call off those two rabid animals.

"You are right. I just got to pray for the best. I think we would feel if she was dead. We would feel it right here. We have that triplet connection. I knew you were still alive." Handsome put his hand over his chest as he stood up and prepared to leave.

"Wait a minute. Tell me something: how did you guys find us? I hope that you were not involved when they were doing whatever dirt they were doing. You have a career to worry about. You are a public figure. Paparazzi would have a field day with your ass." Gigi constantly drilled in her brother's head that he must maintain his squeaky-clean image. In the media, he was adopted. Nobody knew he had siblings or that he was even a triplet. She didn't want what she was doing to fuck up her brother's life.

"They already had been out looking for you guys. Coach K found out where Bea's worker hung out, and they went over there and shot up some cars. Toe-Toe and Nard's homeboy were involved in the shootout with Bea. They found her car off Hollywood Road in front of an abandoned house. She wasn't in it, but it was bloody." Handsome said to his sister as he watched her slide from under Honesty.

"Okay, but how did y'all find us? You are filling in many blanks but not telling me how you guys ended up at the warehouse." Gorgeous felt something wasn't right, and she wanted to know everything.

"Lil' Poke showed up with Bea's computer. It was attached to the surveillance equipment installed in the warehouse, watching y'all. Ponchees knew precisely where you guys were when he brought it in based on how the buildings were positioned. He said that him and Black Sillk used to gamble in that same warehouse a decade ago. We mounted up and came in like the cavalry." Handsome said, smiling.

"See y'all a lil' too damn trusting for me. You know that Bea and Lil' Poke used to fuck around. It was supposed to be a secret, but I knew about it. How do you know he is not down with her? He just walked in with her computer off the street with no problems, and nobody saw this as out of the ordinary. Come on, man. I can't think for all of all of you." Gorgeous got out of bed slowly.

"Where you going, Gigi? Take it easy. You just got shot. I think everybody is still sleeping anyway." Handsome knew that all hell was about to break loose.

"Well, everybody in this muthafucker is about to wake up and answer some questions, and if they don't like what I'm saying or what I'm asking, they can put me out. I got my own damn house to go to anyway." Gigi walked out of the bedroom, leaving Honesty sleeping soundly, and headed toward Coach K's room. She needed some clarity.

Chapter Thirty-One

FROM TIME

Now that her sister was home safe and her brother had begun therapy with his prosthesis, Loyalty hoped everything would finally return to normal. She had decided to sit her family down and officially tell them that she was expecting because, in addition to the slight bulge in her stomach, her face was indeed changing.

She already had her day planned out, which included avoiding Aiden, the doctor. She knew she was vulnerable, and she needed to work on herself. She had too much going on in her life to be trying to date any man. She was still trying to get over the man who had knocked her up. Loyalty had decided today she was going home to her loft. Even though the mansion was humongous, she wanted to be by herself. Honesty and Gorgeous were recuperating; Lil' Poke and Killa were there, and he had a doctor or nurse on duty. Reality and her boyfriend were in and out, and so were Ponchees, Toe-Toe, and Nard. It was just too much, plus right now, she didn't want to be under everybody's prying eyes.

Loyalty went downstairs to find her father and let him know she would be leaving to run errands and then go to her place. As she walked down the hallway with her phone, playing Candy Crush, she barreled into Aiden with her head down.

"You and that damn game. I wish I was as lucky to get some of your attention. I have barely seen you these last few days. Have you seen your brother's progress? He is doing outstanding. Nurse Jones and your other brother have really been helping him." Aiden said to Loyalty as she leaned casually up against the wall in the hallway.

"Other brother? Oh, you mean Pokey? That is our cousin. Actually, we are of no blood relation. His father and our father were best friends. "Everybody had always thought that Lil' Poke was our brother. He and Killa had been around each other so long they started to look alike."

"Wait a minute, I thought that Handsome Diamond was your cousin. I met him the other day. He talked to your brother when he first got his leg."

"Handsome is our cousin, but not really. His mother and my mother were best friends. We grew up together because our parents were the best of friends. They were like siblings. My father is the glue that has always held everybody together.

"That's cool, but to the subject at hand, when will you let me take you out?" Aiden said to Loyalty. He had been chasing her around the house, and this was the first time in days that he had her cornered.

"I got a lot on my plate right now. I'm trying to focus on my upcoming graduation, and honestly, I just got out of a relationship. I'm healing and focusing on me." Loyalty tried to walk past him, but he wouldn't let her.

"Your brother is going to be all right. Your sister is safe now. Relax and enjoy yourself; you are about to graduate from college. You have your entire life ahead of you. Don't stress yourself out. You are living and breathing for two. It is not good for you." Aiden moved out of her path and walked around her toward Killa's room.

Loyalty was rooted in that spot for what seemed like forever. She was stunned. She couldn't believe Aidan knew she was pregnant and was still trying to date her. That said a lot about him. Instead of finding her father, she went into the restroom and looked at herself in the mirror. She had not been for any prenatal care; all she knew was that she was pregnant and that K.J. was the father. Loyalty figured it was time for her to come out of the fog and be honest with herself and everybody else. She pulled up her shirt and looked at what used to be washboard abs. She now had a slight pudge. She dropped her top, turned, and headed toward her father's office.

———————

Coach K heard the knock at the door and told them to come in. He had a migraine that wouldn't quit. His head had been hurting ever since Gigi went on her tirade. He understood where she was coming from, but as soon as things looked like they were returning to normal on the surface, they had other things to face. After all, Beautiful was still out there missing. Blood was found in the car, but she could have just been scraped. And then, he still had to talk to Lil' Poke to find out how he knew where Beautiful lived. He told Gorgeous he had gotten the laptop from her condo right across from where they were found. Lil' Poke just didn't tell how he knew where she lived.

Loyalty walked in, and her father smiled at her. "Hey, Pop's." Instead of sitting in one of the chairs, she sat around the desk in her father's lap. She just needed a hug.

Coach K had meant to talk to his daughter, but he had been so tied up. He didn't want her to think that he had been ignoring her. "Thank you so much for never leaving your brother's side. The fact that I knew he had you taking care of him made this so much easier. Are you ready for your big day? I know I am." He was happy that Killa was working hard so that he would be able to walk across the stage and receive his degree.

Loyalty burst out crying. "I've messed up so bad, Pop's. So, so, so bad, and I don't know what to do. There is nothing to do. I'm stuck."

Coach K hadn't seen his daughter like this since she was little. He should have known something was wrong when she came and crawled into his lap. "It is going to be okay, baby. I promise that whatever is wrong, I will fix it. Don't I always?" He rubbed her back and tried to calm her down.

"I try to be optimistic. Girls my age have had a worse hand dealt to them. But it is hard. I thought I had everything figured out, and then this happened." Loyalty wiped the tears from her face, but they kept coming.

"Baby girl, you are not the first girl that broke up with her boyfriend, and you are not the first girl that a no-good man walked out on when they were pregnant. When I came home from prison, your momma already had your sister. I knew it wasn't my baby; it couldn't have been. I had been locked up for two and a half years. But I didn't say anything. I loved her, so I loved that child. Life for you is not ending 'cause you hooked up with a dumb man. You know for a fact that it is his baby, right?" Coach K looked his daughter in her eyes.

"Yes, Daddy, he was the only one I was with. Wait a minute, how did you know I was pregnant?" Loyalty felt like she had the scarlet letter P on her forehead. It seemed as if everybody knew she was pregnant, but they were waiting for her to say something.

"As long as I'm living and breathing, money will never be a problem, but I will make sure my lawyers bleed him dry. He must not know whose daughter you are." Coach K was going to talk with Sadie. K.J. was raised better than that. He knew it.

"I do not even want him to know. I got my own money, and I know you will all help me. My baby will not need anything at all. Let him be. Karma is my close friend, and she will pay him a visit for this. I know for sure." Loyalty dried the last of her tears. She felt like a burden had been lifted.

"Are you sure you want it like this?" Coach K wanted his daughter to know he was there no matter her choice. She was correct; the child would not want for anything. This family is a strong unit, and it will ensure that the child has all the love, attention, and possessions that they need and desire.

"I'm positive, Pop's. Thank you so much for being an awesome dad. I'm about to go and let my hair down and go to the spa for a massage, a manicure, and a pedicure. I will be heading home afterward. I will call you when I get home." Loyalty kissed her father on his bald head before she stood up.

"No, baby girl, you can't go home yet. Too much is going on. The enemy is still loose. The only reason that Reality can go home is because she and D.J. live together now. If not, she would be here too. I need all of you under my roof to ensure you are safe." Things were not going back to normal until Beautiful and her workers were captured or dead.

"Ugggggggghhhhhh, I feel like a hostage stuck on a luxury compound. Please tell me you are not serious, Pop's. Can I at least do everything else?" She understood the seriousness of everything going on, but Loyalty wouldn't act like she was happy about it. She wanted some time alone.

"Yeah, you can do everything else. Call me when you leave from each place. Take your gun with you, and if you feel that you are being watched or followed, call someone immediately. Be back here by seven p.m.," Coach K ordered his daughter as he reached into his pocket and handed her five crispy one-hundred-dollar bills.

"I feel like a teenager. You are giving me money for the day and telling me when to come home." Loyalty took the bills gladly and placed them inside her purse before leaving her father's study.

As soon as his daughter left, Coach K picked up his cell phone from his desk. "Sadie, we need to talk."

Chapter Thirty-Two

SACRIFICES

Gorgeous was so excited to be able to see Concrete finally. She waited until after the mall opened to go and visit him because she wanted to come bearing gifts. Her godfather had told her that he had him moved to the Shepherd's Center Rehabilitation Hospital because of his injury. She was happy about that; he deserved only the best. She knew that Concrete was going to bounce back. He always did. Gigi knew she was pushing herself a little too far because she had walked all over Lenox Square Mall.

"I think you are trying to do too much at once. I'm about to rent you a wheelchair," Handsome said, going in and out of each store with his sister. He was constantly recognized. He stopped, signed autographs, and even took pictures with some of his fans.

"You know we will be in all the blogs tomorrow, right? I can see it now. Handsome Diamond shops with his new love interest. The new Ebony and Ivory." Gigi laughed as she walked over to Starbucks to get a Matcha Frappuccino, her brother following behind her, carrying her bags.

"I have managed to stay below the radar regarding women." Handsome scoffed.

"You need to be linked to somebody. I know you love the strippers and all. I'm the only one who knows about the pole in your house. The only club you have ever been caught in is Gigi's, and that was just once. In a minute, if you are not seen with a girl, they are going to start saying that you are gay. You need a girlfriend, shawty." Gorgeous leaned into her brother, and when she looked up, she noticed someone taking a picture.

"The last thing you will ever have to worry about is me not liking pussy. I like pussy more than you do, and we know you love pussy. I just got good home management skills. I know how to keep them under control." Handsome knew his sister had many women; he was just surprised none of them had surfaced while she was missing.

"Man, you and I know that your management skills include paying them to keep their mouth closed and to stay under control. If it isn't, tell me what you are doing because that is what I do." Gorgeous made sure everybody she dealt with knew that Honesty came first, and she was always respected to the fullest, no ifs, ands, or buts about it.

"I'm not new to this. I'm true to this. You have to pay the cost to be the boss. Look where we come from; some bosses raised us. Now hurry up so we can go and see Concrete." Handsome took the cup out of his sister's hand and took a sip, and then he caught the camera flashing again. He knew they would be all over the social media."

"Let's go to the Apple store so I can grab Concrete an iPad to keep him entertained. I know he is bored. Damn, they just keep snapping pics. I'm happy that I look a little decent today. I could hardly find anything to wear because of all the weight I had lost. I need to be dropped off at a salon when we leave the hospital. I need a wash and a deep conditioning. I still have some blood in my head that I didn't get out from the explosion. Thank God I don't look like what I have been through." Gorgeous had her hair piled high on her head in a bun. She wore a camel-colored oversized sweater with a pair of black designer jeans that were too big but still looked cute. Gorgeous finished her look with a pair of fox fur-covered Ugg boots and a matching scarf thrown around her neck.

"Girl, you got nine lives." Handsome followed her into the Apple Store. He had decided to buy Concrete the iPad and some Beats headphones. He walked in front of his sister and went straight to the Genius bar, where he was recognized immediately. That is what he was hoping for. He was thankful that he was a celebrity for that reason; he didn't stand in any lines.

"Look at Mr. Big Shot, alrighty then." Gorgeous put a pair of Beats headphones and a case on the counter as her brother told the young man that he wanted the 256 GB iPad Air.

Handsome swiped his Black American Express card and signed a personalized autograph for the young man who helped him. He said he had been a big fan since Handsome was in college. "Can we please leave the mall now, ma'am? I'm begging you."

"Yes, we can. I need you to make one more stop before we get to the hospital." Gigi always could get her brother to do anything for her, even when they were kids. He was always at her beck and call.

"I hope it is not in a store. You know you got more money than me, right?" Handsome was kidding with his sister; he liked being home with her and buying her stuff. She had helped support him financially while he was in college.

Gigi rubbed her hands together, smiling devilishly. "No, we are going to Cami Cakes. That is everybody's favorite, especially Concrete."

After getting dozens of cupcakes from the infamous bakery, the brother-and-sister pair headed to visit Concrete. They rode the short distance in silence. Gigi was unsure of what she was going to see. Her brother had told her that Concrete was awake and that he was not on any type of machine, but he wasn't the same. She was scared; she didn't know what she would do if he never walked again, especially since he had been injured, saving her life.

They went to the information desk and found out what room he was in. Gigi wanted to surprise him, so she told her brother to go in first, sit down, and talk for a few minutes, and then she would walk in.

Handsome agreed. He entered the room carrying balloons, a card that Gigi had picked out, and the bag from the Apple Store.

"Hey bro, how is it going? I haven't seen or heard from anybody since I got transferred over here. I thought y'all had forgotten about me again." Concrete was happy someone was there to visit him. He adjusted his bed so he was sitting in an upright position. All he had been doing lately was staring out the window. He didn't even turn the television on.

"Ain't nobody forgot about you. You know we can't do that. It's getting hectic out there in the streets, though, I ain't lying. I'm ready to get back home. ATL ain't the same anymore. For all the glitz and glamour it has, it is filled with violence. You can't even look at the news anymore. I know it is everywhere. Stuff happens up there where I'm at, but here it hits home cause it's somebody you know, or somebody some kin to someone you know. This younger generation has no regard for people's belongings or human life in general." The things he had seen since he had been back home saddened Handsome.

"Why do you think I have my television powered off? They are shooting up schools, breaking into houses, and killing mothers and children. We ain't no OGs, but some raised us. These folks don't have a code anymore. You don't take from the hard workers. You don't hurt your neighborhood, no women, no children, and no senior citizens.

This generation is lost, and there are no leaders. Everybody is a follower, and now they are gangbanging. Shit is really ridiculous. We only banged green, and the only set we claimed was our neighborhood."

"You damn sho' right, bro. I'm happy I got away, but looking at this generation makes me want to return and do something to help. They need to see that there is more to it than what they see. It is getting out of hand." Handsome sat down in the chair beside the bed.

Gorgeous sat outside the door and listened to the two men talk. It made her want to return to her old neighborhood and do something positive. She would start to brainstorm about that later.

Concrete looked at all the balloons and the card Handsome had brought into the room with him. "Thanks, man. This room needed something to brighten it up. When I got hurt last time, I had so many flowers and balloons in my room that Gigi had sent every day that I started to give them to other patients on the floor to lift their spirits."

"Yeah, man, I remembered that. Gigi was going hard then. She was walking around like a chicken with her head cut off. You were laid up in the hospital, and Black Sillk was at home dying of cancer. She was determined to do double duty. She was with the both of you every day. She came and sat with you and read to you every day when you were in a coma." Handsome knew his sister was the definition of loyal. She went to bat for everybody she loved. He just hoped she still had some love for their other sibling when she was found.

"She is amazing. I feel like I have dishonored her or abandoned her somehow. If I'd been there, she wouldn't have gotten kidnapped. I am her protector. You know that it was the last thing Black Sillk asked me to do was to protect his baby girl, and I failed. She could be lying somewhere dead. Beautiful doesn't have a heart; she wants to be her, and she wouldn't have a problem erasing her permanently so she can take her place. I failed her miserably." Concrete sobbed quietly with his head down.

When Gorgeous heard how hurt Concrete was, she walked in the door. His quiet sobs shook his body. She placed the bag on the floor and the Cami Cakes on his serving table and wrapped her arms around him. Tears flowed down her face. "It is because of you that I'm here. You never failed me, and don't you ever think you have."

Concrete looked up, and when he locked eyes with her, he knew that this was Gorgeous. He couldn't stop the flood of emotions that hit him when he saw she was okay. He wrapped his arms around her tightly and almost picked her up from the ground. He let her go and said, "I swear I have never been so happy to see somebody in my life. You are truly like a vision from above." He then wrapped his arms around her again.

Gigi laid her head on his shoulder. Handsome was her brother, and they were born together, but Concrete was that friend that they spoke of in the bible who would be closer than a brother or sister. "Man look at you; you have gotten all skinny and shit. You got hair on your head, and your beard hasn't been trimmed in God knows when. Let me get your barber over here." She took out the cell phone she had just purchased and realized she didn't even have any numbers on it.

"I know I look rough and I've lost weight but everything is right in my world because you are okay." Concrete felt on top of the world, he felt like he could get up and walk out the hospital right now.

"I was heading to the salon, but I really need to go by the club. I will send the barber over here who usually cuts your hair. I have to make sure all my babies are all right. I hope that bitch ain't ran my club in the ground with the both of us gone." Gorgeous said as she got up off the bed. She felt a little pain on her side where she was shot. She touched it lightly and felt moisture. She looked down and saw her sweater had a bloodstain on it.

Concrete noticed the grimace on Gigi's face, and he saw her touch her side, then he noticed the blood. He screamed, "What the fuck happened to you?"

Gigi hadn't gotten around to telling Concrete what had happened when she got kidnapped. He wasn't allowing her to. Even though he wasn't on any monitors, she didn't want him to get upset to make whatever was wrong with him worse.

"Beautiful, did this? I'm going to kill that bitch with my bare hands." Concrete knew he had to walk again. He had a mission to accomplish.

Chapter Thirty-Three

TOO LATE TO APOLOGIZE

Killa sat on the edge of the bed and rolled a blunt. He had started to smoke heavily lately, but it was the only thing that eased his mind. He tried to put his best foot forward and be brave but was broken inside. He had lost Leigh, and he had been refusing to see Kaydence because he didn't want him to see him without a leg. It was bad enough his face was scarred; he didn't want him to see him messed up.

Lil' Poke knocked lightly on the bedroom door and then entered. "Damn, my guy. Are you rolling another one? You need to cool out. When don't you get high?"

"When I'm sleeping. Smokin' on Purple, ease my mind," Killa sang the lyrics to one of his favorite Lil' Boosie hits. His nurse was about to come in and start his physical therapy session, and he had to get his mind right first. It fucked with him every time Killa looked at the nurse who reminded him so much of Leigh. It also fucked with him every time he strapped on the prosthetic leg.

"I can dig it. I'm happy you decided to keep your nurse. Your pops told me that she looks just like your lady and that you wanted to fire her at first. I don't know what it is, but she works magic on you. I can tell she is very passionate about physical and mental therapy. She makes sure that you stay optimistic about your situation and about you walking every day." Lil' Poke could see his attitude change since he began his intense therapy.

"I appreciate you helping me out. This is a struggle, but I got to do it. I'm determined to walk across the stage and get my degree. I know that is what Leigh would've wanted. They are doing a special tribute for her at our graduation ceremony. My lil' man is going to be there. I got to be in tip-top shape. I told him that I would see him at the graduation. I hope I'm mentally ready to see Kaydence without cracking in front of him. I miss the hell out of him. I was going to ask his grandmother if he could spend some time with me after graduation. When are you going back to Cali? Are you going to be here for the graduation?" Killa was surrounded by girls so much that he was happy that the guys had been crowding him lately. Plus, when he was by himself, he had visions of Leigh and nightmares of the accident.

Toe-Toe peeped his head in the bedroom door as Killa got off the bed and walked across his bedroom with the blunt in hand. "What it do, lil bro? I believe you will be running faster than me in a minute. If I didn't know it from watching over here, I would think you were Shawty, the pimp who walked with a limp."

"We got some unfinished business to take care of. Gigi approached me all hyped up, asking how I knew where Beautiful lived. She was talking crazy like I was down with Beautiful after knowing she was the reason why my pop was dead and gone. I understand she is suspicious, but she needs to calm down with the accusations." Lil' Poke was ready to get in the field, solve some problems, and clear his pop's name. He had to find Beautiful. His contact, who had located her in the first place, had not had any luck yet. She had not been home, and she had not had any bank or phone activity. It was like she disappeared into thin air. There was blood in the car, a lot of it, but he didn't think that she was dead. Two weeks had passed, and no bodies had been found. He had been checking the morgue every morning.

Both men had concluded that Poke was just a puppet on Beautiful's string. They were not blaming Lil' Poke for the shit that his father did because the drugs had changed Poke. But they also were not trying to rehash everything he had done. They were trying to get past all of it, and the first thing on the agenda was to get ahold of Beautiful. Just like a snake, the body shall perish if you cut off the head.

"She pulled a disappearing act, but Pop's ain't going to let it fly. Shit is not going to be right until she found. He is going to hunt her down like a dog. Now, he always wants everybody under him because he doesn't know when Beautiful will pop out like a Jack in the Box. I'm pretty sure there will soon be a mutiny on the bounty. We are all grown and used to going and coming as we please. Even though I am not trying to go anywhere, I don't want to be told when I can come and go." Killa passed the almost finished blunt to Toe-Toe.

"Nigga where you trying to go? It ain't like you got a girl or some-thing." Lil' Poke said before he realized what he was saying. When he looked up, Killa gave him the ice grill, and Toe-Toe was wide-eyed.

"Right, I don't! But I'm going to kill everything living that had something to do with me losing the one that I had." Killa limped out of his bedroom, leaving Toe-Toe and Lil' Poke inside.

He limped down the hall as fast as he could, tears falling from his eyes. He looked at his Rolex. The nurse was scheduled to be there in less than thirty minutes. This would be his first time going outside to walk. He was ready because he needed the fresh air. He didn't care how cool it was. He pulled the hood of his black Polo sweat suit over his head and opened the door to sit on the steps.

Lil' Poke felt bad; he didn't mean to say what he had said. It slipped out before he knew it. He couldn't imagine what Killa was going through, but he knew the pain ran deep. "I'm sorry, I didn't mean what I said." He said as he walked out the front door and approached Killa from behind.

"Nigga, I lost my lady and I lost my leg. It ain't shit that I can do with your I'm sorry!" Killa didn't turn around.

Chapter Thirty-Four
SITUATIONSHIPS

Sam had literally been on pins and needles since the funeral and shooting. She could not locate Beautiful and knew that finding her would be the only thing to make Ponchees stop the silent treatment. He acted like she was the one who shot up the damn funeral. Sam wished that he would just take his ass back to Mexico cause his being here but not being with her was killing her.

Sam got out of bed slowly, regretting staying up late the night before. She and Rafek were out riding around the city looking for Beautiful. Focusing on finding Beautiful was preventing her mind from drifting to her problems. She was trying her best not to think about her brother harassing her for information or her surprise pregnancy. Sam wished that she had some friends besides Rafek and Ponchees. She didn't have any girlfriends to talk to. Her mind drifted to when she first met Gorgeous.

Her stomach growled, and she decided to eat today. She had been starving herself, eating only salt-and-vinegar potato chips and drinking Sprite because it was the only thing that stayed on her stomach. She didn't just have morning sickness; she had all-day sickness. Maybe it was time that she went to visit her doctor. Sam knew it had to be something that they could prescribe to keep the food on her stomach.

As soon as her feet hit the floor, the bile started to rise in her stomach. Sam rushed to the bathroom, vomited in the toilet, and brushed her teeth. She put on a comfortable matching athleisure set and UGGS to match, ran her fingers through her bob, and headed out. It was still early; Sam hoped that her gynecologist's office wasn't crowded. Needing alone time, she didn't call Rafek to join her. He was her constant shadow, but Sam would do breakfast alone today. She had a lot to think about.

She parked her Bentley coupe in the parking deck and walked through the adjacent building to her doctor's office at 285 Boulevard. Her stomach growled something awful, but after vomiting up all the foam this morning, she decided to lay off the Sprite for a while.

Sam didn't realize how early it was until she turned the knob on the door to the doctor's office and realized that they were not open yet. She remembered passing a vending machine downstairs in the medical building's lobby. She got on the elevator, silently praying they had something salty, like plain chips or pretzels, that she could snack on. The salt in them settled her stomach.

The door was unlocked when she got back to the doctor's office. Sam went inside and signed in at the registration desk. There was only one other patient in the waiting area. She sat down, snacked on the pretzels, and sipped ginger ale. Soon, other women started coming in, many of them in different stages of pregnancy. She wondered how she was going to look pregnant. The way things were going, she wondered if she would even go through with the pregnancy. Her name was called, and she folded the bag of pretzels up and dropped it in her purse. She put the empty soda can in the trash and followed the nurse, who took her into an exam room.

The seconds turned into minutes, and the minutes had turned into an hour as Sam sat on the exam table in her paper gown, waiting for her gynecologist to enter the room. She finally walked in, her blue-black waist-length curls trailing behind her.

"Hello, I'm Doctor Maria Aiello," she said as she extended her small hand toward Sam.

Sam burst into giggles. She had been coming to this practice since she was a senior in high school and had been a patient of Maria's since she finished her residency and joined the practice alongside her father. She was happy that a woman had joined, especially one with small hands. Men could be so rough, even when they were not trying. "I like that new hair color. You are rocking that."

"Thanks, girl, you know I have to do stuff to keep me young 'cause God knows I don't have time for a social life outside of work. All I do recreationally is shop and get pampered. I get fly to come in here and look between the legs of dozens of women daily and deliver babies. But anyway, please tell me what brings you in here. It must be important. You walked in." Dr. Aiello and Sam hit it off during her first visit, and ever since then, she has only seen Maria.

"I'm pregnant," Sam blurted out. This was the first time that she had said those words. It felt like a ten-pound weight had been lifted off her shoulders. Now that she had come to grips with it, she just had to figure out what she would do.

"Wow, really? How do you know? Talk to me. What has been going on? And is it by Big Daddy? You know, I think y'all are so cute together." When she was on a date, Dr. Aiello had seen Sam and Ponchees out to dinner at Ruth Chris Steakhouse.

"Yes, it is by him. I have morning sickness; as a matter of fact, I have all-day sickness, and I took a pregnancy test because my cycle was late. The test was positive, of course, and then my boobs are sore as hell." Sam couldn't believe that she had gotten pregnant after being with Ponchees for all these years. She didn't even think he was fertile.

"Well, it sounds like you are pregnant. I'm going to examine you and then read your labs." Dr. Aiello put on her rubber gloves and examined Sam from the rooter to the tooter.

Her assistant knocked at the door and handed her a slip of paper. She looked at the paper and then looked at Sam.

Sam could tell by the look in her doctor's eyes that she was indeed pregnant. She looked like she didn't know if she wanted to congratulate her or apologize. Honestly, Sam didn't know how to feel. "Can I put my clothes back on?" she asked.

"Yes, you can, ma'am. Go sit in the waiting room, and one of the nurses will call you when it's time to take your ultrasound."

"Ultrasound? Isn't it too early?" Sam's heart immediately began to race. She really was pregnant.

"Do you have any idea how far along you are? When was your last period?" Dr. Aiello questioned Sam, who looked like she was on the verge of tears.

"I...I... I... don't know. I can't remember. I have been under a lot of stress these last few months. I have to remind myself to eat some days. Speaking of eating, I haven't had a complete meal in about two weeks. Can you prescribe something to help with the nausea and vomiting?" Sam couldn't remember the last time she had a period, but she did remember that it was only for a day when it came.

"Yes, I will prescribe you something. The tech will be right out to get you. Everything is going to be fine. Quit worrying."

Sam returned to the waiting room and twiddled her thumbs. She wanted to call Ponchees and tell him the news but decided against it. He was giving her space so she would grin and bear it. He would come around soon enough—at least, that was what she hoped. He was her best friend and her partner; she hated not being able to talk to him about everything.

"Loyalty Rasheed, Dr. Aiello is ready for you." The nurse said from the doorway.

Sam turned around when she heard that name and watched as Coach K's middle daughter got up and followed the same nurse who had come to get her. It was a small world, and Atlanta was even smaller. She reached down in her purse and fished around for her cell phone. Sam hadn't seen it since placing it on silent the night before because of her brother's nonstop calls. She had eighty missed calls and fourteen text messages when she pulled it out. She scrolled through and noticed Ponchees had called her over fifteen times within the last twenty minutes. The rest of the calls were from her brother and Rafek. Sam decided that she would give him a taste of his own medicine. After confirming her pregnancy, she needed an off day.

———————

Shocked beyond belief, Sam sat at the gas pump with her head on the steering wheel, crying. She couldn't believe Dr. Aiello had just said she was pregnant with twins, not one baby, but two. What in the world was she going to do? The gas pump clicked to let her know it was finished, but she did not move. What were tears had now turned into full sobs. Her body shook as she cried hard for the first time in years. She wasn't ready for one baby, much less two. God was definitely a comedian. Maybe he was mad because she didn't talk to him enough.

There was a tap on the window, and she looked up, expecting to see a junky begging for change. Instead, it was Loyalty Rasheed with a carton of chocolate milk in her hand.

"Are you okay? I saw you leaving the doctor's office but couldn't get your attention. I just stopped to get some gas and noticed you here crying. Whatever it is, it's going to be okay. I firmly believe that if you say it enough, it shall be. Just pray about it. Allah never puts more upon your shoulder than he has equipped you to bear." Loyalty opened the carton of milk and stuck the straw in it. She was craving chocolate like it was going out of style and hoped she wouldn't start experiencing breakouts.

"Thank you so much for checking on me, Loyalty. I also saw you, but I didn't know if you were trying to be discreet, so I didn't bother you." Sam wiped her tears away and smoothed back some strings of hair that had fallen into her face.

"You didn't answer my question. Are you okay? Do you need me to call Ponchees or your bodyguard? Girl, you are sitting in the Fourth Ward in a drop-top Bentley. I know you are strapped and everything, but this is not where you want to sit still and have a sob session by yourself." Loyalty had to remind Sam where she was; like her father said, even if you got a gun, you are still a woman.

Sam noticed her fuller face and the small pudge in her belly. "Are you expecting, too? Is that why you were at Dr. Aiello's office?"

Loyalty reached into her Birkin bag, pulled out her first sonogram picture, and held it up. "Yes, ma'am, I'm about to be a mother and a father." She laughed to keep from crying as she looked at the picture of what would soon be her child.

"Well, at least it is only one." Sam held up her sonogram, which had spots on it, which the doctor determined to be two embryos.

"Oh my God, Congratulations! Ponchees is going to be so excited. He is old enough to be a grandfather and is just now becoming a father. I'm sorry. I didn't mean to say it like that, but you know what I mean. I just saw him at our house last night." Loyalty said, wondering why

Sam had not been with Ponchees all the times that he had been at her house. Honesty had told her that Sam was his business associate and his woman.

"I know, he might as well move in. I need a drink. Shit, I can't drink." Sam's stomach rumbled so loud that she looked down at it. When she looked up, Loyalty was looking at her stomach as well.

"Girl, it sounds like you need something to eat. I know I do. I'm about to head down the street and pig out at my favorite breakfast spot. Then I'm going to get my hair and nails done." Loyalty had just gotten her hair and nails done less than a week ago, but she was doing anything she could not to be a hostage in the house.

"Please take me with you." The doctor had given her some samples of the Phenergan, and she felt like she could hold something on her stomach.

"Okay, you can follow me. We will make a left on North Highland at the light." Loyalty got into her Porsche truck and headed to Highland Bakery with shrimp and grits on her brain.

Chapter Thirty-Five

PARDONS AND PAROLES

Ponchees sat in the den with Coach K. The private detective had just left after briefing them on his search for Beautiful. "I think she is dead, I really do. We have had an eye on her phone lines, credit cards, banking accounts, and condo, and there has been nothing, zero, zilch, nada. Gigi said there haven't been any unfamiliar transactions on her accounts since she came home."

"I won't believe she is dead until I see a body. It is going to take a little bit more than a bullet-riddled car and some blood to make me think that lil' evil bitch is dead. Bitches like that don't die anyway. She will probably live until she is one hundred years old. "Coach K's cell phone vibrated, and he looked down; it was Jazmeir. He still was avoiding her. He had bigger fish to fry right now.

A text message popped up after the phone stopped ringing. I'm going through Poke's things. I was contacting you to see if you and his son could come by to see if there was anything that you guys wanted before I donate it all to charity.

"I bet her people know where she is. We need to go back over there, and this time, we need to knock on some doors." Ponchees said, talking about the guys who worked for Beautiful.

"Dem some Westside niggas, I wrote the rule book for the game. You shoot first and ask questions later. We can't knock on nobody's door and expect them to come out to politick, especially after we sprayed up their rides. I know they are trained to go." Coach K was wracking his brain trying to figure out how to lure them into his neck of the woods or a way where he would have home-court advantage.

"We gonna think of something 'cause y'all can't live in a state of paranoia all the time. Especially from Beautiful, it's bad enough you got to be wary of the police and the robbers, but damn, this child is going in for no reason at all. I still, for my life, cannot figure out why she got a vendetta against your family. I know why she is like that about her sister. She never liked her."

Ponchees had no idea why Beautiful was warring with Coach K and his family. He needed Sam to use some of her resources. He decided now it was time to take her off punishment. Besides, he had been missing the hell out of her. He dialed her cell, and there was no answer. He dialed it several times before putting his phone back in his pocket. It seemed like she was trying to ignore him now.

Honesty walked into the den and sat down on the sofa. She was tired of reading books and lounging around. She missed being in the thick of the streets. Her time around the house had given her some time to strategize. She didn't plan on selling dope forever, but she damn sure didn't plan to stop right now. Gigi had already told her that she had a warehouse full of dope waiting. She was ready to get back in the game. She hadn't been in contact with any of her workers. Her dad told her everybody was suspect. Honesty was ready for this entire situation to be over and done with. She wanted to put a bullet in Beautiful herself. She had basically pushed the pause button on her life. There had to be something she could do. She exhaled loudly on the sofa, clearly restless and irritated.

"I didn't say you couldn't go nowhere. I just said keep it limited. Do what the other girls are doing, get your hair done, or go shopping. You gotta take somebody with you. You can't be alone." Coach K felt like a warden to his children.

"Loyalty doesn't have anybody with her. Why do I have to have somebody with me?" Honesty pouted as she got up from the sofa. She headed to her brother's room to see if he had a remedy for this problem.

"Nobody has it out for your sister personally. You are a target. Get over it, Honesty." Coach K shouted as his daughter stomped from the den, her shoes sounding loudly against the hardwood floors.

She tapped lightly on the door and then twisted the knob. The door was locked. She turned and walked away.

"Who is it?" Killa asked as he took the gun apart to prepare it for cleaning.

"It's me, Honesty. You busy?" She said

Killa got up, opened the door for his sister, sat back on the side of his bed, and continued cleaning the pistol.

"You getting ready for a war I don't know about?" Honesty asked as she watched her brother break down pistol after pistol and clean them methodically.

"I'm up and walking now. The graduation is coming up, and I will see my little man. I want to be able to look in his eyes and know that I did something to avenge his mother's death. I'm going to get that bitch Beautiful. I know how, but I don't know where. I really wanna snap her neck so I can actually feel the life leave her body. Look in that top drawer over there and get that weed and roll us a blunt." Killa said to his sister as he started to put the guns back together.

"I swear I was just thinking that. My life is literally at a standstill. Pops won't even let me go outside. We need to get rid of this bitch for good. What are we going to do because she is deep in hiding now?" She rolled the blunt like a pro and lit it with the lighter that her brother handed to her. She inhaled the weed smoke and choked. The tears poured down her face as she tried to catch her breath. She didn't know if it was the fact that she hadn't smoked in a while, but the weed was strong as hell.

"Good shit, huh? We are connected and have resources; she can't hide from us. She will turn up when we least expect it, and I will be ready to knock her block off. I'm going to torture her. You got to know it's some consequences and repercussions for all this shit that this bitch thinks she has gotten away with."

"I know Gigi is plotting on the low. She just ain't saying nothing. Even though this is her sister, I don't think she will let her get away with it. They not only share the same face but also the same DNA, but Beautiful hates her sister. That is just pure evil. I love all y'all no matter what stupid shit that y'all do." Honesty handed her brother the blunt and watched his hands work in amazement. Their father had shown them all how to clean their guns, but her brother's hands were moving fast, putting the parts back together like he was a machine.

Killa blew perfect circles into the air. "I'm going to talk to her later on. We got to come up with a cohesive plan to go ahead and get this over with."

"Retaliation is a must!" Honesty said, mimicking her father.

Chapter Thirty-Six

WHICH ONE YOU WORKING?

D.J. had just left his auto repair shop. He was headed to his jeweler to check if the ring that he had designed was ready. Now that Honesty and Gigi were back safe, he knew there was no time like the present to go ahead and pop the question. He had fallen in love with Reality, and it seemed she had swept him off his feet instead of vice versa. Now, his life had a purpose. Every move he made, he thought of her and their future first. His cell phone rang loudly; her face popped up on his screen.

"Hey baby, what are you doing?" Reality said a singsong voice.

"Just out taking care of business. I should be ready to head to your father's place in about two hours." Coach K made sure they checked in with him every evening. He didn't mind. He was so used to being by himself all his life that he was happy to see his new family every evening. They all sat around and talked or ate. He felt included and had to admit it felt good to be a part of something.

"I'm so tired of reporting. I feel like Pop's is our probation officer.

But I'm happy that I come home to you because everybody else got it really bad. It's like I'm on supervised probation because of you, but everybody is still locked up. With you, I can come and go as I please," Reality said as she got up and stretched. She had been sitting at the computer all morning working.

"It ain't that bad, baby. I don't mind. It's coming from a good place. Your dad wants to make sure everybody is A-1 at all times. It doesn't get any more stand-up than that."

"When you see your Baba later, can you stop at the wing spot and grab me some wings? Those things are the bomb." Reality hadn't eaten all day. She walked into the kitchen and grabbed an apple off the counter. Hopefully, that would hold her until she got the chicken wings from her favorite place.

"Okay, baby, I will get them on my way to pick you up. Let me know if you need anything else or if you leave the house before I get back in." D.J. made Reality's safety a priority. He knew that her dad trusted him with her, so he did his best to ensure that nothing happened to her. He knew what he had signed up for. She wasn't just a regular girl from a regular family. She was this beautifully intelligent woman from a family considered royalty where he came from.

D.J. made it to Solomon Brother's jewelers in record timing. He hoped he didn't get caught in the Buckhead traffic because he still had to see Chief. He exited the elevator on the seventh floor filled with excitement. He had purchased a Tiffany engagement ring but wanted a larger diamond placed in the setting. He was dressed for Buckhead today. A non-descript designer buttoned-down shirt with a corduroy blazer, dark denim jeans, designer high-top sneakers with no jewelry, only his presidential Rolex.

Even though D.J.'s wardrobe was noteworthy, he hardly ever went anywhere. All he did was grind, whether in his trap house, his auto body shop, or the studio he was building. His scars made him not want to draw attention to himself. He was happy with fading into the background. D.J. knew that even if his face weren't scarred, he still would probably be the same quiet, humble person. But he knew it was bigger than just him when he stepped out. He was representing his girl and everything that she represented.

Solomon Brothers treated all of their customers like they were spending millions of bucks, and that is what he loved about them. He was escorted to the back, and Frenchie greeted him with a smile.

"I got you all ready, my man. When are you going to propose? Do you have something special planned?" He turned around and headed toward the vault to retrieve the ring.

D.J. had been thinking about how he would ask her, but he hadn't come up with anything special. He would talk with her father first and ask for his youngest daughter's hand in marriage. After receiving his blessing, he would propose to her in front of her family. Just keep it plain and simple. He just hoped that she liked the ring. He knew for a fact that she loved Tiffany & Co. jewelry. She had a boatload of it already.

Frenchie returned with the small blue velvet box partially open in his hand and handed it to D.J., whose eyes lit up with satisfaction. "What do you think?"

The ring was perfect. The diamond looked more prominent now that it had been set. The cut and clarity were excellent. He was very satisfied. He reached into his back pocket, pulled out his Louis Vuitton wallet, and put his Amex on the counter to pay his remaining balance. Frenchie swiped the card and printed a receipt. D.J. signed it and handed back one copy to him. When he looked down, he thought the television stars were lying about their wedding rings, or Frenchie had given him a good deal. In all, the ring was almost thirty thousand dollars.

"I know she is going to love it. Thanks, man. You know I will be back." D.J. shook Frenchie's hand, put the blue ring box in the inside pocket of his blazer, and headed toward the elevator, a happy man.

Reality's eyes hurt, and she was tired of figuring out this mess. The refund checks had stopped flowing. She still had her other revenue streams flowing in, but Brian had been hounding her to find a way to get around what the IRS had in place. She hadn't so far, and she was tired. Her phone rang, and Reality immediately picked it up and regretted it. It was Brian; she wished she had looked at the caller's I.D.

"Hey, let's have lunch. I have some business to talk to you about." Brian wanted to know what else she could do and what she had her hands in because his money was drying up. He was spending it fast as it came in. He knew she had other things up her sleeve and wanted in on it.

"Can't do lunch today. I got so much work to do." At first, he seemed okay, and their business relationship was cool. Then, she started to feel very unsettled about him whenever she was in his presence. She just couldn't put her finger on what it was. She didn't talk to D.J. about it. She never even discussed that her new connect was a male, because she knew immediately what his reaction would be.

"Well, let me assist you with your work 'cause God knows I don't have any right now. Put me on like I put you on." Brian lived by the two mottos, 'You only live once' and 'Blowing Money Fast.'

"Shiiiiiiit, that is a lie. You've been in the game long enough to realize you must keep more than one iron in the fire. I know when shit is going too good, it can dry up at any time. You might have reached the end of the road with this one, buddy. But it was good while it lasted." Reality wanted to end this business relationship with him and leave on a high note. The way things ended always determined if there would be any leftover animosity. She did her best to maintain good business relationships. You never know when someone will turn snake because you have left them feeling some type of way. She knew you couldn't trust any niggas, especially after what happened to her father and his right-hand man.

"You're right; I think this shit has dried up too, so that is why I need you to plug me in on what you got going on. I'm just happy the Feds are not hitting hard up here like they are hitting down there in Florida. All my old crew is gone. I'm happy I relocated when I did." Brian said to Reality. He knew that she had other shit going on. She had almost twenty workers who depended on her to live; she had to make something happen for their sake.

Reality's facial expression changed when he said something about the Feds and Florida. She had forgotten that was where he was from. D.J. told her that she needed to move all the work from the home office to somewhere else because he had seen something on CNN about how the Feds were working with the police in Florida, taking down people for taxes. He said that down there, they had stopped selling dope, and everybody was eating with the taxes. "Hey Brian, I'm going to call you back. I just remembered something."

She immediately went to the hall closet and pulled out two empty Nike gym bags. Reality proceeded to dump in legal pads, prepaid credit card information, fake identifications, W-2s, 1099s, social security cards, and everything she had gotten from Brian over the past few months they had worked together. She dumped in her iPad, an HP laptop, and one of her MacBook Airs. Her gut told her that something wasn't right, and she was going with it.

She packed all her stuff in the other bag for her regular business. Brian only knew about the residence she shared with D.J. He didn't know about her condo. She planned on working from there from now on. D.J. didn't bring work home, and neither would she.

She got the two duffle bags, slipped her Ugg boots over her leggings, adjusted her sweater, grabbed her purse and pistol, and headed out the door.

Chapter Thirty-Seven

BED PEACE

The Doctor and the nurse stood over her, removing the tape and taking the tubing out of her nose and mouth. Beautiful looked at them, frightened. Her gray eyes bucked with fear. She didn't know where she was, what had happened to her, or how long she had been like this. She could barely turn her head from side to side because of the way the tape and tubing were in place, but she knew that she was not in a hospital. She hated not knowing what was going on. Tears ran down her face. The nurse stopped what she was doing. She thought removing the tape hurt Beautiful when she saw the tears. She smiled down at her reassuringly, moistened the medical tape with a warm, damp sponge, and started to remove more of it. It came off easier that time.

The Doctor tugged on the tubing gently until all of it was removed. Her throat was so dry that it hurt. She needed to cough, but when she attempted it, her entire diaphragm felt like it was on fire. She just wanted to know what had happened to her.

"Water, water, please?" She begged, barely above a whisper. Her mouth felt like it was drier than the Sahara desert. Her tongue felt like a thick slab of sandpaper against the roof of her mouth. Her stomach growled loudly, and the nurse smiled at her.

"We will get you something to eat as soon as we get you cleaned up. I promise you can have whatever you want. The Doctor wants to ensure that your plumbing is still intact so we can start you with some liquids and soft foods. You are blessed to be here. The bullet did not hit any of your vital organs. We didn't see an exit wound, and the Doctor could not locate the bullet." The nurse said to her as she removed the remainder of the tape from her face.

"Where am I?" Beautiful looked around, panicked. She didn't recognize the room.

"You are at home, ma'am. Let me get your husband," the nurse said as she left to locate Mr. Ball. He was in the living room talking to the Doctor. She approached quietly to allow them a chance to finish their conversation.

The Doctor turned to face her. "Nurse Jones, what do you think? You are more up-to-date on conditions like this. Do you have any suggestions regarding the next course of treatment for the patient?" The Doctor was a general practitioner. He was not afraid to admit that he did not have as much emergency medicine experience as she did. He was happy that he was able to do something to save this patient's life. He had not been faced with a life-and-death case in over twenty years.

"I'm going to be honest, Doctor. Mrs. Ball really needs to have a CT scan. I know we had the portable X-ray machine bought in, but without her having an exit wound, we do not know what type of internal damage has been done. She can feel her limbs, so we know she isn't paralyzed, but she still may have some nerve damage. I will do all that I can, but I suggest she go to the hospital." Amor had been wracking her brain, coming up with scenarios for how this young lady was shot and why her husband didn't want to take her to the hospital.

All the clues continued to point to the husband as the one who did it. She watched how he doted over her, so she thought that it had to be an accident, and he was scared to take her to the hospital because he was going to be charged. Rich people thought that money could help them out of everything.

The Doctor looked at Tristan and waited for his response.

"Well, you said that you would try her on liquids for twenty-four hours, and if she did well, then you would move her to soft foods. If there is a problem after that, I agree with her being hospitalized. But I believe she will be better than she was before."

He honestly, for the life of him, could not figure out what had happened that night he rescued Beautiful. Tristan just hoped that whoever was after her that night had given up their quest to kill her. It was more than evident from the bullet-riddled Phantom that they were shooting to kill. He didn't think that she was going to make it, but her last words before she fell unconscious were not to take her to the hospital, and that is what he was doing, keeping his word.

Tristan's past life in Port Au Prince and Miami had put him in a position to understand that the authorities weren't always necessary. He couldn't play Inspector Gadget right now because he was focused on getting her back to healthy. He would find out who was after Beautiful as soon as she was better and eliminate it and them. He got up and followed the nurse back into the bedroom after the Doctor had left. He sat in the chair beside the bed and softly rubbed her hand. The nurse was changing her IV to her left side because the vein had collapsed, and she had told the Doctor that she wanted to be able to use her right hand.

"Who are you?" Beautiful asked the nurse as she taped the tube to her arm.

"My name is Amor, Mrs. Ball. I am your private duty nurse."

She looked at the man rubbing her hand. "And who are you?"

"Baby, you don't know who I am? It's me, Tristan." Tristan let go of Beautiful's hand, stood up, got the cup of ice water from the nightstand, and put the straw to her lips. He watched as she sipped. He rubbed the top of her head soothingly. She was obviously suffering from some memory loss. He wondered what could have caused that because she didn't have any head trauma.

"Well, Tristan, who am I?" Beautiful asked. She didn't know these people, what had happened to her, or where she was.

Amor panicked; it was apparent that the patient was suffering from memory loss. She had seen this happen dozens of times when she was in combat. It was more than likely caused by her traumatic experience. The brain was truly like a computer. It had shut down to protect itself during stress. Some patients' memories came back automatically after a short period of time, and others took longer. They came back after being around people and things they were familiar with from their past.

"Don't worry, Mr. Ball. Everything will be okay. This happens more than you could imagine." Amor said.

Beautiful didn't like them talking like she wasn't there. "Please, can one of you tell me who I am and how I got here? What happened to me?"

———————

Over the next few weeks, Beautiful slowly healed from her injury. Her memory still hadn't returned, but there was also another unexpected side effect.

Tristan sat at Beautiful's bedside and rubbed his hand over his bald head. He was scheduled to return to work today but didn't want to leave her side. She was doing much better than when he first brought her into his home. He was no longer worried about her health. The Doctor said that she was going to be okay. He wondered when her memory would return because he liked the new Beautiful. Hell, he was falling in love with the new Beautiful. She was peaceful, kind, soft-spoken; she was beautiful inside and outside.

The nurse was coming over earlier today. She had arranged to have an assistant join her so that Beautiful would have someone there with her at all hours since he was returning to work and the nurse had other patients to see.

Beautiful stretched her long limbs, moaned, and rolled over. Tristan was in his usual spot, sitting in the chair at her bedside. She noticed the worry on his face. "Baby, what is wrong? You are supposed to be excited to go back to work. There is only so much you can do from home. Please thank your colleagues for all of their well wishes. It means a lot. When I start to get up and around, I'm first coming to the office to thank them personally."

He shook his head and smiled. He didn't want the old Beautiful back; this one, right here, was perfect.

Chapter Thirty-Eight

MR. BENTLEY

Coach K sat up at his desk when D.J. walked in. He had just ended a phone call with Mrs. Sadie. As if he needed more bad news or enemies, she had informed him that K.J. knew everything or at least most of it. The things that he didn't know, he was on a hunt to fill in the blanks. It seemed like, for the last past three months, Coach K had been in the middle of a shit storm. He straightened up his face because he felt the frown from the previous phone call.

"Good evening, Coach. Do you have a few moments? I have something that I would like to ask you." D.J. walked into the study and sat in the chair facing Coach K.

"Even if I didn't, for you, I would make time. What has my baby girl done this time, son?" Coach K smirked. He had grown to love the young man his daughter had fallen in love with. He knew that his youngest daughter could be more than a handful. She was the feistiest of all of the girls.

D.J. reached into his blazer pocket and pulled out the small blue box. "Sir, I want to ask you for your daughter's hand in marriage."

Even though the priest had told him to wait a while to propose, he would do it anyway. The priest had told him today that Reality's work might get them both in trouble and that he needed to eliminate her business partner because he was a snake. Reality didn't mention her business associates often; all D. J. knew was that they were Haitian. He had planned to talk to her on the way to her father's house, but she had told him she would meet him there tonight because she had some last-minute business to take care of.

A big smile spread across Coach K's face. He needed this good news to brighten the dark mood that the conversation with Sadie had put him in. He really didn't want to open that closet with those old skeletons. "Son, not only would I give you her hand, I give you all of her. You are the best thing that ever happened to her. I don't think that I could have picked a better man for my baby. Welcome to the family." He got up from behind the desk, gave D.J. a handshake, and embraced him tightly.

D.J. could honestly say he had never felt better a day in his twenty-seven years of life. He couldn't wait until he presented Reality with the ring and asked her to marry him before her family. It was as if her love had erased his past. He didn't have nightmares anymore. He didn't think about the scars on his face; he no longer thought about his lonely childhood. This was the first time in his life that he felt like he belonged to anything. This was the first time that he had a family. "Thank you so much, Coach. It is truly an honor. I promise to continue to protect and provide for her and put her and whatever children we have first. You have my word. I will die for your daughter."

"Not Coach, call me Pops like all my other kids. Wait a minute, what children? Is Reality pregnant? Is that what this proposal is about?" His eyebrow shot up as he looked at D.J. with apprehension.

"No sir, she is not expecting. She doesn't even know that I'm here asking you this." D.J. reassured him.

"I knew I was saving those bottles of Ace of Spade for a good reason. I think the entire family is going to be here tonight. We are celebrating the future nuptials." Coach K patted D.J. on the back as he headed out of the study to answer the ringing doorbell. He was expecting Ponchees. He had called him to tell him about the call from Sadie, and Ponchees said he was on his way over.

Coach K opened the door, and Loyalty stood there, fishing in her purse with Sam at her side. "I couldn't find my key, Pop's." Loyalty said as she held up the ring of keys, she had finally located at the bottom of her purse at the last minute.

"Well, I hope you can locate your pistol while standing outside in the dark fishing for some keys. Hey Sam," He said, moving to the side and letting the girls in. He wondered to himself how these two had ended up together. He said nothing and returned to his study when the doorbell rang again. He exhaled loudly and turned around to answer it. Coach K didn't know if it was the stress of everything that was going on or his old age, but he was tired.

Handsome and Gorgeous walked in the door that Coach K held open. He acted like he was the butler. He stayed close to the front door long after they had walked away from it in case the doorbell rang again. Just as he moved to walk down the hall, the doorbell rang again. He held his hands up in the air and exhaled loudly. "I'm going to hire another housekeeper. I can't do this shit all day." He opened the door, and Ponchees stood on the other side of it.

"You look like you are tired, my brother." Ponchees said as he walked in the front door and patted his dear friend on the back.

"I don't know if I'm getting old or all this shit going on is wearing me out. I can tell you one thing: a vacation is coming up. I might just come to Mexico and chill with you for a while. I need to get away. I'm not about to stroke out, worried about all this shit." Coach K said as he followed Ponchees into the den.

I hope you got some food on the way, old man. You got a house full of folks and no groceries. It's dinner time." Handsome said, taking a bite out of an apple that he had brought from the kitchen.

"A house full of adults. Y'all are responsible for your own meals. I fed y'all enough growing up. Now answer the door." Coach K said as the doorbell rang yet again. It seemed like he had sent the bat signal up. The house was filling up with all his loved ones. He wasn't going to complain.

"Where are the menus for the restaurants that deliver out here? I know you have all of them because you are a bachelor. I will take care of the tab."

The doorbell rang again. "There is a menu for a new seafood spot called Louisiana's Kitchen in the drawer on the island. Hurry up and answer the door; I'm tired of hearing the doorbell ringing," Coach K said.

Handsome went to open the door before retrieving the menu. His stomach growled loudly as he opened the door, and standing there was the young lady from Poke's funeral. She was holding a safe.

Chapter Thirty-Nine

RIDE FOR MY MUTHAPHUCKIN' NIGGAS

"So your nurse let you leave from in front of the door? She acts like she is your bodyguard." Nard said jokingly as he pulled the blunt and passed it to Killa in the passenger seat.

"Well, big bro has been coming over, and he has been buttering her up. She thinks we are going to the gym to play basketball." Killa said as he hit the blunt and held the smoke so it could enter his lungs.

"His ol' prince charming ass. He has that effect on all the women. Everybody trusts him but his girl. She swears he be out doing wrong." Nard said, talking about his big brother.

"All I do is talk nice, act respectful, and respond to all questions. They feel they can trust me because I have nothing to hide. Y'all should try the shit. It gets you places. Girls run the world." Toe-Toe said as he headed down 85 South back into the city. It felt good to have Killa out with him. He didn't know what Killa had up his sleeve until he got to the house to pick him up. He was the oldest of them, and he usually would be rational, but he knew that this was something that Killa had to do himself.

"What is the plan? Man, we haven't rode on no niggas in a long ass time. We got young niggas to do this type of shit, lil bro. We are basically some made men. All we are supposed to be doing is sitting back and making cash. Let me call my young gunnas and tell them to get ready. You know they stay on go. Let them handle this." Nard told Killa, trying to encourage him to change his mind about handling this situation himself.

"Money can get shit done, this I know for sure. But you know that I'm that nigga that other niggas pay to handle they shit, right? I'm a killer. I don't need y'all to ride for me. I need y'all to ride with me, literally. I just needed to leave the house and not raise a red flag. Y'all call drop me off at my spot, and I can jump in my car and handle this shit by myself." Killa did not plan to sleep until he got Beautiful. He had been going hard in therapy and the in-home gym. He was back near one hundred percent, or as close as he would be with a prosthetic leg. His graduation was next week. He was not going to look in Leigh's mom's or Kaydence's face without knowing that he had done all he could to avenge her death.

Toe-Toe saw that Killa was getting irritated. "We are not about to drop you off so you can go alone. We are with you, lil' bro; we got your back. Let's go and make these niggas tell us where this bitch is at." He pressed the accelerator harder, and the 1996 Impala Super-Spor' coasted down the highway at full speed.

"Y'all ain't got to act like I'm boo-boo the fool. I know you already had this planned. Toe-Toe, you ain't drove this damn car in god knows when. You got on all black. You were ready to ride." Nard looked at Toe, and Killa dressed in all black in the black car with the dark tint and figured they already had this planned. They looked like they were ready to go and get their hands dirty.

"I swear this ain't nothing but a coincidence. I'm in the Marauder because I went and got it serviced a little earlier. Somebody asked to buy it, and I refused, but I have been letting it sit and dry rot. I got to start driving it more often." Toe-Toe said to his brother, who he noticed was looking at him with a side-eye.

"Whateva man, I'm an O.G. we're too old for this shit," Nard said as he sat back and folded his arms across his chest.

"Either get the hell out or shut up, nigga. I'm riding for Killa, point blank, period. End of story." Toe-Toe said adamantly. He was not about to let Killa do anything alone and was tired of his brother complaining about it. Having all the workers had made him soft and lazy.

"I'm with y'all regardless. I'm just saying tho'," Nard said as he exhaled loudly.

Toe-Toe got off the highway at the Bolton Road exit. He had to stop on the hill to get some artillery. He walked in the door, and Rich was in the kitchen with his shirt off and gun in his waist. Toe-Toe could see that he had taken off this bandage. Rich had scraped his elbow and shoulder to the white meat when he shot up Beautiful's car. He jumped and dived out of the way of her car onto a mound of rocks, gravel, and cement. He had less severe scrapes on his hands and knees as well.

"What's up, bro? Y'all ain't hear nothing bout dat bitch Beautiful yet?" Rich didn't know if she was dead or alive. He just knew that he had emptied his pistol into the Phantom and that she was alive when she tried to run him down.

"Shit, we are about to go and get some answers right now. Killa found out where the niggas hang at that shot up the funeral and kidnapped Gigi dem." Saying that out loud made Toe-Toe realize he had to ride with Killa. These same niggas could have killed him, his brother, or his mother when they shot up that funeral.

Toe-Toe entered the closet and got a Tech 9, AK-47, AR-15, and a sawed-off shotgun. He already had his 45 on his hip.

"I'm riding with y'all then. You know how we do. Where is O.G. at?" Rich asked, asking about Nard. He wore a T-shirt and pulled the black Nike hoodie over his head. He reached under the cushions on the sofa, got out a nine-millimeter, identical to the one already on his hip, and put it in the pocket in front of the hoodie.

Both men headed outside, with Toe-Toe locking the door behind them.

"So where are we headed?" Toe-Toe said to Killa as they rode down Hollywood Road.

"The old Suburban Court," Killa said as he pulled out his chrome Glock 40. He was ready to do some damage.

"Martin Luther King and Fulton Industrial?" Rich said aloud to no one in particular.

"Yeah, that is where my pops said the nigga who works for Beautiful spot is. Some big black nigga name May-May." Killa said.

The other three men in the car looked at one another. They were all familiar with him. Rich grew up in Bankhead Court, where he used to hang out. A lot of the young niggas that he had working for him, he was cool with. He continued the ride in silence. It was family over everything. Toe-Toe and Nard were his family, and Killa was theirs, and that was just how it was.

Nard knew that he claimed Bankhead Court, so he looked over at his homeboy. "If you have a problem with this, we can drop you off."

Toe-Toe looked at the interaction of the two of them in rearview. He waited in anticipation at the red light. He didn't have a problem letting Rich out. He understood that just because he was their enemy didn't mean he was Rich's enemy. But he was from the old school, where the whole family had the same enemies.

"I'm good, y'all riding on a nigga; I'm riding with you on that nigga, too," Rich said.

"Dats right too," Killa said. He didn't know much about Rich other than he was a significant part of their team. Toe-Toe and Nard fucked with him heavily. If they trusted him, he did too.

"He got a lot of young niggas with him tho', this I know for sure," Rich said, thinking about all the boys that hung around May-May, some of whom he had hung with or watched grow up.

"I ain't trying to kill an army of niggas. I just want to kill the general. If you get the head, the body will perish. I want this nigga; I couldn't care less about the rest of them. But I got some hot for them if they run up." Killa said as they turned into the apartment complex. He remembered that when he was little, these apartments were abandoned. He didn't even remember them opening back up because he never traveled this far down Martin Luther King, Jr. Drive.

"Pull over to the other side between these buildings. That is May-May spot over there." Rich pointed to the apartment at the very end of the building.

"Leave the car running, I'm about to wait on the side of the building for him to come out, and I'm going to knock his block off. Y'all just stay here and watch my back. If you see them other niggas, y'all know what to do." Killa got ready to get out of the car.

"Wait a minute, bro. We need to snatch this nigga up. He can tell us where Beautiful is. She is the head." Toe-Toe said as Nard nodded in agreement.

"You right, that was my objective at first, but then I started to think about how this is the nigga that shot my pops and that kidnapped my sisters. I need him to talk to tell us where Beautiful is, but I'm still going to kill him. Who bout to help me get his ass then?"

Nard didn't give the other two men time to decide; he immediately opened the car's back door and got out with Killa. Those bullets flying at the funeral could have killed his mother.

The two of them crept around the building quietly, pistols at their sides. The streetlights in the apartments had been shot out, so people could not see who was coming and going. The only light they had was the half-moon in the cloudless sky. The apartment was at the end of the building, which was perfect. They could stuff him in the car and leave right out of the apartment complex.

When they got to the edge of the building, they stooped down and waited patiently for him to come out. Hopefully, it will be sooner than later. They had been waiting for less than five minutes when Nard felt the barrel of what could only be a pistol on the back of his head.

"Fuck!" he muttered aloud as he shook his head. He couldn't believe that he had gotten caught down bad like this.

"Yep, you niggas played pussy, and now you are about to get fucked." Lil' Poke had two pistols drawn on the men waiting outside.

"Pokey?" Killa recognized his best friend's voice.

"Killa? Nigga, oh, so you weren't going to call me to ride with you?" Lil' Poke said as he drew back the two pistols he had pulled on them. He looked at Killa and Nard, who had turned around and mean-mugged him after he pulled the pistols back. They were coming for a war, but they didn't look like they were ready to battle. They were dressed in all black and had on hoodies, but he was equipped for a war. He had on a bulletproof vest and a ski mask. He had planned on leaving these apartments and getting in his car just as he walked in, without a scar.

"Nigga you didn't call me either! We will talk about all of that later. Let's get this nigga so we can find this bitch." Killa didn't feel like arguing or debating with Lil' Poke about why he chose not to call him.

"Aight, but we are going to talk. The big nigga just went in with two duffle bags about fifteen minutes ago. I've been here for about two hours. I was about to get him when he was going in, but one of the niggas on the inside came out to the car and got one of the bags." Lil' Poke didn't care how long it took. He was getting this nigga today. He had been lying on his belly in the shrubbery right outside the building, waiting for him to come out by himself.

Nard was trying to come up with a plan in his head. He hated doing anything halfcocked. He looked at Lil' Poke, and he had to admit to himself that the young boy looked like he came to put in work. He was trained to go. "What is he riding in? I heard their rides got shot up."

"He in that black SRT8 over there." Lil' Poke pointed at one of the two vehicles parked in front of the building. "I got it. This is what we are going to do. I'm about to go and see if the doors are unlocked. Y'all watch my back. If they are unlocked, I'm getting in. Then y'all go back, jump in the car with Toe-Toe and Rich, and follow him wherever he drives. I'm going to lay low until he is out of the complex. Then, pop up, he won't know what hit him.

"I need to look this nigga in the eyes. I need to see his fear. I'm getting in there with you." Killa said to Lil' Poke.

Nard sat silently and saw Lil' Poke's temple start to jump; Killa was doing the same. He felt the tension in the air. It seemed like they were about to pounce on each other. "Aye, both of y'all calm down. Lil' Poke is the fastest of the two. I suggest that he run and get in the truck. You can get in Killa when they pull out of the complex. If that nigga got a gun to his head, trust me, he is gonna do whatever he is told. Lil' Poke will make him pull over for you to jump in."

They looked at each other and agreed silently.

Lil' Poke ran around the building and tried the back door to the SUV, which was indeed open. He got in and crouched down. Nard and Killa stayed on the side of the building with their guns drawn, waiting for him to come out.

Chapter Forty

SUPER RICH KIDS

"To think I used to complain about the house being empty and me being lonely." Coach K said aloud to no one in particular as his house buzzed with various conversations here and there. He had not had a house full of people like this in years. This is the type of activity he had in mind when he helped design the house all those years ago.

Reality had just walked in, given D.J. a kiss, and then sat down amongst her sisters. He loved seeing the three of them together. Sam sat there with them and blended right in. Coach K noticed his friend was still giving his girl the cold shoulder. He looked over at Jazmeir, who sat on the ottoman Indian style by herself. They locked eyes. He didn't expect her to show up at his door. He didn't even remember telling her where he stayed. But truth be told, he did so many things at once and communicated with more people than usual. He might have said it in conversation. He was unsure. Now that she was in his house, he would have to talk to her. She made him feel like a teenager, and she didn't even know it.

Sam got up from where she sat with the girls talking and walked over to the bar where Ponchees was fixing a drink. She didn't say anything at first. She just leaned her body into his. All she wanted was for him to wrap his arms around her. Sam inhaled his scent into her lungs. She had been missing her man. She couldn't imagine her life without him.

"Without you, there is no me. Please stop hurting me like this. I have enough going on. I need you." She whispered into his ear.

His arms lingered at his side until she heard her whisper that she needed him. He wrapped his arms around her tightly. He missed her softness. He knows he probably missed her more than she missed him. This girl had a hold on his heart that was not getting any looser. "Te he echado de menos y Te amo," Ponchees whispered in her ear.

Sam wanted to melt, hearing him say that he missed her and loved her. She figured now was as good a time as any. She reached into her handbag and pulled out the ultrasound she had taken. Her heart was pounding in her chest from the nervousness. "Baby, I'm pregnant," Sam said as she handed him the first picture of their two unborn children.

Ponchees jerked back with his eyes bucked like a snake had bitten him. The first thing that came to his mind was that he was too old to have children. The second thing he thought was that he was too old to have children. The third thing he thought was that he was too old to have children. He then looked down at the ultrasound and squinted. This was not the first time that he had seen one. Why did it look like there were two heads? "Is it two babies right here?" He asked as he looked up at her, shock and awe on his face.

"Yes, it is," Sam said, looking at him and trying to read the look on his face.

Ponchees took her face in his hands and kissed her deeply. Now he knew why she had been so emotional lately. It had to be the pregnancy hormones. "I'm about to be a dad. This is the best gift that you could have ever given me. I love you so much, Samantha Jones."

———————

Lil' Poke, Killa, Toe-Toe, and Nard came in through the back door of the house and crept up the back steps quietly. When they got up the stairs, each of them went their separate ways on the second and third floors of the house so they could get cleaned up.

Toe-Toe closed the door quietly and went straight to the sink. He took a deep breath, turned on the hot water, and scrubbed his hands. Although he didn't do anything, he felt dirty and still had a lot of residue on his hands from the rubber gloves. He had been in the streets a long time, practically all his life, and he had never seen as much blood as he had seen tonight.

He was worried about his lil' homie. Nard sat on the toilet with the seat down and pulled out his phone to call Rich. Even though he didn't say anything during the entire ordeal, he could tell that he had a major problem with it. But he knew for sure that he wouldn't ever utter a word because Lil' Poke had scared him shitless. He put the phone in his back pocket when he didn't get an answer. He removed his shoes and put them in the sink with the soles up so the hot water could rinse the blood and dirt. Nard then put his shoes back on his feet and dried them off on the rug. He washed his hands repeatedly in hot water and splashed some on his face before he walked out of the bathroom towards Killa's bedroom.

Killa came out of his shower. He had stripped naked and put all of his clothes in a trash bag. He had already thrown the gun away that he had used. He looked at himself in the mirror and didn't look any different, but he felt different. This wasn't his first time murdering someone, but this was the first time that he had murdered someone on his behalf, and it wouldn't be his last. He had to get Beautiful if it was the last thing that he did.

The nigga wouldn't give up Beautiful's whereabouts. Killa shook his head in pity. May-May had died trying to save a bitch that probably wouldn't pass him the salt across the dinner table. He guessed he didn't know she was only out for herself. If she were in the same situation, she would've pointed them out and taken them to the executioner. He found out the hard way that loyalty isn't shit if all parties are not loyal.

It was sad to say that this was the first time since Killa woke up from the accident that he felt whole. It took him to get his hands dirty for him to feel like Killa Rasheed. Something about holding a person's life in your hands made you feel invincible. He entered his bedroom and closet and put on another polo sweatsuit and a pair of Jordan XI Gamma Blues. A knock on the door just as he was tying his shoes. "Who is it?" He called out as he shut his bathroom door.

"It's me." Coach K said with a grimace on his face. His intuition was never wrong when it came to his children. His son was up to something.

Toe-Toe and Nard met in the hall and headed toward Killa's bedroom. They both saw Coach K and wished they could run back downstairs and hide like some kids.

Nard tried to play it off, "Man, I'm getting old. The young boys on that court got me tired as hell."

"Hell yeah, we got to start doing that more often, 'cause we going to fuck around and dry rot just sitting up. I know I felt rusty out there today. It was like I never played before." Toe-Toe said as they approached the bedroom door as Killa was opening it.

"What's up, Pops?" Killa said as he moved out of the way as his dad barged in. He looked at the back of his head as if he was crazy.

"Shit, you tell me. You are sneaking in your house now and have the get-along gang with you." Coach K said to his son as he looked around at the three of them. All of them had guilt written all over their face. He didn't know what they were guilty of.

Chapter Forty-One

FROM BIG DOG TO LIL' PUPPY

Lil' Poke stood under the double showerhead and let the scalding hot water beat his skin. Still no Beautiful, after all that had happened today, still no progress on finding her.

When the SUV pulled out of the apartment complex, Lil' Poke put it to the back of the driver's head. He squeezed his long frame from behind the seat and sat comfortably on the back seat. He expected the big dog to start barking, but instead, he started whimpering.

"Please, my nigga, don't kill me. You are a little late. I don't have any money or work on me. I just dropped it off at the spot."

Lil' Poke used his other hand to reach over the passenger seat and grab the pistol May-May had laid on the seat when he got in the truck.

"Trust me, my dude; I ain't trying to get you for that lil' bit of chump change you got or the poison you are pumping. Where is Beautiful?" He cocked the pistol so he knew that he was ready to shoot him.

"I... I... I... I... I don't know. I haven't talked to her in a long time." he stuttered.

Lil' Poke looked in the rearview and saw Toe-Toe following behind them at a safe distance. "Pull over up here in the Park West driveway. And don't try nothing funny."

As soon as they pulled over, Killa jumped in the front seat of the SUV. You could barely make out who he was because he had the hoodie pulled so far down on his head. "Pull out, my nigga; I will tell you where to go. Be calm. All we want is some information." Killa pulled his hoodie off his head, and May-May's eyes bucked in fear.

He immediately started begging for his life. "Please, my nigga. I don't know anything. I ain't talked to Beautiful, I swear. Whatever you want, I can give it to you. Don't kill me; I got children; I got a new grandbaby on the way."

"Nigga, you got children walking around looking just like you that you ain't seen in years. That children's card is one that you can't play. When was the last time you talked to her? Where did you see her last? Who was with her when you saw her last? Who else is working with y'all?" Killa was firing off questions back-to-back as May-May drove up M.L.K. in silence.

Lil' Poke looked forward, and all he could see was the fear in the driver's eyes as he remained silent. "Nigga you don't hear him talking to you? Tell us something, speak up."

Killa looked at the gas gauge and saw that the SUV had a full gas tank. "Well, I'mma be honest, I got a lot of time, and you got a lot of gas. I can ride around all damn night with this gun in your face, ready to bust if you don't give us something. Hop on the highway up there."

"So we are going to ride around 285 all night? I don't have time for all of that." Lil' Poke said to Killa as he pulled a straight razor and leaned close to the driver.

"Oh, nigga you can't hear him talking to you. Let's see how good you hear those children and grandchildren talking to yo big azz without ears." He grabbed his ear and cut it off the side of his head so fast that he didn't know what was happening to him.

The scream that ripped through the car was gut-wrenching. Blood spewed everywhere as May-May reached up with one hand and held the spot where his left ear once was. He tried to remain calm and keep his other hand on the steering wheel as they headed north on 285.

Lil' Poke tossed the bloody ear in his lap. "You see that. You got one more. Tell us where Beautiful is right now. You are already funny-looking. You won't be able to get no hoes walking around without ears. That shit ain't cute." He laughed demonically.

Killa thought to himself that this nigga had to be dumber than he gave him credit for because he still was not giving up any information on Beautiful. So he decided to switch gears. He needed them stationary. He glanced in the rearview to make sure that Toe-Toe was still following them. "Get off on South Cobb Drive. Let's take this nigga back to his spot. I don't think that he knows anything. Leave him alone; don't cut his other ear off." He wanted to fool him into trusting him.

"I 'preciate it, my nigga. I really don't know anything." May-May said, half relieved that they were about to let him go. He didn't know who the nigga was in the back seat that had cut his ear off; that didn't matter to him. He knew that he was affiliated with Killa. He was going to make sure Killa paid for him losing his ear, and he was going to find out who this nigga was in the ski mask. He planned on him getting it even worse than Killa was.

Lil' Poke knew that Killa wouldn't let him off that easy. "So you just going to let him get away with all the shit he has done. Man, let me out of the car. As a matter of fact, pull over right now and let me out." They were traveling up Bolton Road.

"Pull over right here and let this nigga out," Killa said as they were about to pass Chattahoochee Park. He was ready to finish what he came to do. He was not telling them anything about where Beautiful was.

May-May pulled over into the dark park and wished that he hadn't. There was nothing he could do. He had two guns pointed at him, so he just complied. When the back door opened, he breathed a sigh of relief. They really were going to let him go. He saw another set of lights pull in behind him but noticed that they didn't panic. It was more of them. "Please don't hurt me. I can pay you. I told you I don't know anything."

Lil' Poke quickly snatched open the front door, almost snatching the handle off the door. "Oh nigga you know something, and I'm about to find out everything. Killa, let me get that front seat so I can chat one-on-one with our friend here."

Killa backed out of the car slowly, never taking his gun off May-May. Lil' Poke got in the front seat when he got to the other side. He had no idea what he had planned. Killa was still in shock that Pokey had cut this man's ear off and threw it in his lap.

"Aye, you can shut the door. I want to have a one-on-one with our little friend. I think he will feel more comfortable without you standing there watching him." Lil' Poke said to Killa.

May-May's heart dropped when Killa shut the truck door and walked to the car behind them.

"How are you doing, my nigga? I asked him to leave because you might feel a little pressure, you know him being Coach K's son and all.

I really just want to find Beautiful. I'm not trying to harm her. I'm trying to save her. That is my first love, and I want to get to her and get her away from all of this before they get to her cause I know they are going to kill her. So tell me where she is. Oh, and sorry bout dat lil' ear thing," Lil' Poke said nonchalantly.

Toe-Toe let the window down when Killa walked up to the car. "So what is going on, Lil' Bro? Is he talking or what?"

"Nawl, he keeps saying that he don't know where Beautiful is," Killa responded to Toe-Toe.

"I might have to go up there and help Lil' Poke work the info up out of him. I need to hit the nigga with my pistol or something. He did shoot at me, my momma, and my brother," Nard said from the passenger seat.

"If anybody can get the information out of him, it's Pokey. His torture game is unbelievable. I kinda think the nigga don't know where Beautiful is seriously. Pokey already cut his ear off." Killa laughed, thinking May-May didn't stand a chance with Lil' Poke.

"Damn, what made him cut the man's ear off?" Rich asked from the backseat.

"He was acting like he couldn't hear us. I wanted to punch his ass in the face. I hate to be ignored. But that nigga cut his ear off so fast I didn't know what happened. All I heard was his fat ass squealing like a Pig, and then Pokey threw the ear in his lap." Killa said, thinking about the look he saw in Lil' Poke's eyes in the truck.

Nard opened the door and stepped out of the car. "I'm bout to go and see what the hell going on up here."

A loud shrill went through the air as they approached the truck. It sounded animalistic. Both men looked at each other and jogged the short distance to see what was happening. Nard opened the door, and blood was everywhere. He expected the nigga to be dead, but instead, May-May was clutching his left one, and blood was flowing like someone had turned on a faucet.

"What da hell?" Nard asked, trying to figure out what was going on. He looked past May-May and looked at Lil' Poke with the straight razor in his hand. He then noticed the index finger in May-May's lap beside his ear. He shook his head and backed away from the car. He didn't think he was ready for this shit that Lil' Poke was on.

Killa saw the look on Nard's face and bent down to look in the truck. He saw tears and snot running down the man's face; he had children his age and was crying like a baby. Lil' Poke was punishing him.

"You have lost a finger and an ear, and you still not going to tell us where your girl is? You gotta know she wouldn't be down for you like you are for her. This man's daddy was working for her just like your punk ass, and she burned that man alive. That bitch ain't loyal. You have fucked up, but you can redeem yourself. You got clean cuts. They can sew your lil' ear and finger right back on." Killa said to May-May as he watched him cry in pain.

He sniffled loudly and then turned and looked at Killa. His eyes were begging him for mercy. "I swear I don't know where she is. I've been trying to find her, too. I don't know where to look, which is the god honest truth. If y'all let me go, me and my team can help you find her."

"Yeah, right. You and your team are going to help us. The same team that kidnapped my sisters... The same team that shot up the funeral where my pops got shot, and innocent people could have been killed. I know you know where she is; this is my last time asking you this. Where is Beautiful?" Killa said, hitting the back of the seat that May-May was sitting in with frustration.

"I ain't gonna keep telling y'all I don't know where she at." He replied with an attitude. He was tired and pissed off.

Killa pulled the trigger, sending pieces of his face flying all around the front of the car. Blood and matter landed on the windshield, and Lil' Poke jumped back in surprise, but not before a clump of his face landed on him.

"Well, looks like we are done here." Lil' Poke said as he got out of the truck.

"Yup, but still no Beautiful," Nard said quietly as they returned to the car.

Chapter Forty-Two

MEET ME AT THE ALTAR

Loyalty walked down the hall. She was going to her bedroom to have a few minutes to herself. She was surprised by the house full of people. It reminded her of when she was a little girl. Although she already knew she was pregnant, it was something about having the ultrasound done that made it real to her. She had heard her baby's heartbeat. After her graduation, she planned to vacation for a little while. She might go back to the west coast with Pokey. She needed a change of scenery.

"So, are you ready yet?" Aidan said as he saw Loyalty coming up the hall. He was walking through the house to find Killa. He would be officially discharged from his care next week.

"Ready for what? In my life, I don't have to be ready for anything. It just happens. I never have time to prepare." Loyalty said as she looked up at Aidan. His blue eyes were so clear. They reminded her of diamonds.

"For me to take you out on a date. Nothing serious. I just want to get you outside of the confines of your home, to get to know you." He replied to her as he leaned against the wall. She looked even more beautiful than she ever had. Today, her hair was not in a ponytail. It hung down her back, almost touching her waist. She had on a small amount of make-up, but it only enhanced her natural beauty. There was no doubt about it. She was beyond beautiful to him.

"I told you before, I don't have time to date. I have a lot on my plate, and you know this. So don't apply pressure." Loyalty said as she walked past him.

"I'm not applying pressure. We do not have to date. I don't know what you will tell our children when they get older and ask about before we were married." Aidan called after her seriously.

Loyalty almost stopped in her tracks, but she didn't. She continued up the hall, hollering, "Bye, Aidan."

She threw herself on her bed, took out her phone, and looked at the pictures of her and K.J. when she was visiting him in Florida. Loyalty looked at the smile on her face; she knew her heart was smiling, too. She had never been that happy before and didn't think she would be that happy with a man again.

Coach K still didn't know what was happening with his boys, but he knew it was something. He had to handle this situation with Jazmeir. He walked over to her and grabbed her hand. She pointed to the safe. He bent down, picked up the safe, and carried it to his office. He was filled with apprehension. The way things had been going on around him, he did not doubt in his mind that the bottom would fall out when he opened the safe.

When they walked into his study, Jazmeir closed the door. She sat down as he put the safe on the desk and sat in his leather executive chair. "I've never had a man run from me. If my heart hadn't already experienced so much pain, I might have been able to say that I was heartbroken."

He inhaled and exhaled loudly, "I'm sorry, Jazmeir. I truly am. That was not my intention. I just have so much going on that I'm trying to get a handle on. Please forgive me."

"You have been avoiding me as if I was the plague. Do you blame me for the things that Poke did? Is that what it is? I would understand guilt by association." She said as she crossed her legs and sat back in the chair.

He didn't know what to say, so he just decided to be honest. "You know you are beautiful, strong, intelligent, loyal, sexy, and honest. You are everything that any man could ever want, including me. But you are Slow Poke's ex-girlfriend and Black Sillk's baby momma, and I have kids your age. I didn't know how to handle that. I thought staying away would make me not want you, but it hasn't. I think about you every day. Sometimes I think of you, look down, and you call my phone. I want you without a doubt, but I feel funny because my best friends are your exes."

"Both of them are dead and gone. We are here amongst the living, and we want to be together. I can't speak for Poke cause he was not right, but do you honestly think Black Sillk wouldn't have wanted us to be together? When he was diagnosed with stage four cancer, he started trying to get me to go on dates with men before he died so that he could approve of who his son would be around and who would take care of me. I know for sure that he would've picked you." Jazmeir was sure of that, but then again, she wondered why he had never brought Coach K around, even though he always talked about him. Maybe he knew that she would want Coach K.

"You are right. They are no longer here among us. But what about the age difference? I know my children will have a fit." Coach K always had to consider his children's feelings.

"All of them are here, am I correct? How about I go in there and ask them how they would feel if I dated their father." Jazmeir got up from her chair and headed toward the door. She wanted this man and was about to let it be known.

"Wait a minute, I thought you came here for the safe." Coach K said as he got up from his desk to follow her.

"What I want isn't in the safe. You are what I desire," she said, not paying attention to where she was walking, almost running smack dab into Lil' Poke. Her face flustered immediately. She suddenly felt bad and decided not to say anything to Coach K's children, especially with Lil' Poke here.

"The water in the Chattahoochee has not yet taken my dad upstream. Can you wait? Damnit man. On to the next one." Lil Poke shuffled past Jazmeir, looked at Coach K, and then walked into the den, where it looked like a party was happening. He had just put the clothes in his backseat. He was about to go and dump them, along with the blades and the knife. He just wanted to make sure that Killa had gotten rid of everything. He locked eyes with the guys and motioned for Killa to come over to where he was standing.

"Yo, what's up?" Killa asked Lil Poke, noticing his nurse coming in the door. She looked around like she was looking for him.

"I'm about to go and get rid of everything. I advise you to do the same. We ain't leaving no evidence." Lil' Poke said as he followed Killa's gaze to his nurse.

"Aight, wait a minute. I need you to get the clothes." Killa didn't know where she was headed, but he wanted to make sure she was not going to his room. He walked over to where she was.

"Hey Killa, I left my iPad here earlier. I just came back by to get it.

You know that I'm not going to be here tomorrow. But I'm sure you can handle yourself without me." Amor was so proud of Killa and his dedication to getting back to his former self. He had surprised her because, at first, he acted like he hated strapping on the prosthesis.

"Yes, I should be good. You know that I'm never alone. Thank you for your hard work and dedication to my treatment. You were here to be my nurse, but you wore many hats. I want you to know that I appreciate you."

"Aww, thanks; I'm happy you are doing much better. Me and the doc's last day is next week and then you are on your own. Don't forget what I told you. You are done with physical therapy; now, you need mental therapy. Trust me, it will make your life so much better. I know it will help with those nightmares." She smiled at Killa. He appeared so resilient, but she knew he woke up in sweats or crying out for his girl-friend most nights.

"How do you know? You are a little Miss Perfect. Your textbooks can't help you with my nightmares." Killa hated it when she and the doctor told him that he needed to see a counselor.

Amor bent over and pulled up her pants leg. She glanced up, and Killa's eyes had doubled in size. She pulled her pants leg down and stood up. "Trust me when I say that a car accident can't amount to the shit I have seen over there. At least you fall asleep and are awakened by a nightmare. Try not even closing your eyes, and the nightmares still come. I know about counseling because I used to need it every day; now, I go once a week. I sleep like a baby when I do sleep, though." She left him staring behind her with a look of shock still registered on her face.

D.J. stood up from where he was seated, and he looked at the crowd of people who were scattered here and there. "Can I have every-one's attention? I didn't plan any of this, but it couldn't be any more perfect because everyone important is here."

Reality looked around and saw her father, her two sisters, her brother, Lil' Poke, Gigi, Handsome, Ponchees, Sam, Toe-Toe, Nard, Jazmeir, the nurse, and the doctor. Then she looked at D.J. as he reached into his pocket and pulled out a small blue box. Reality recognized that color blue anywhere.

"I would like to thank all of you for welcoming me into your family. A lot of you don't know my story, but my mother died when I was a very small boy in a house fire, the same fire that I was injured in. I never knew my father. My grandmother raised me until she died, and instead of going into foster care, I decided to take care of myself. I have never had a family and never felt like I belonged anywhere or was a part of anything until now. I want to thank all of you for making me a part of this unit." D.J. felt tears threatening to come from his eyes.

He got down on one knee in front of Reality with the blue box. "Reality Skye Rasheed, will you marry me?"

Reality leaped up and wrapped her arms around him, almost knocking him over. She screamed, "Yes, Yes, Yes," as tears poured down her face.

Seeing her so overwhelmed made him emotional. The tears finally sprang from his eyes. D.J. picked Reality up off the ground and kissed her deeply.

She broke the kiss and said, "Now put me down, and let me see what kinda of bling you got for your queen."

Everybody burst into laughter as D.J. put the ring on Reality's finger.

"Time to celebrate. Let's pop some bottles." Coach K hollered over everyone as they congratulated the couple. He had brought up three bottles of Ace of Spades from the wine cellar downstairs.

"Wow, did your boy tell you he would do that? The wedding is going to be bananas, Honesty is going to be a bridesmaid, and you are going to be the best woman." Handsome joked with his sister, who laughed but then clutched her side in pain.

"Damn, I have started back bleeding again. Let me go and change my bandage and my shirt." Gigi said, trying to do it quickly before Honesty saw it. She didn't want her worrying; she couldn't handle worry like the average person.

"Man, you are still bleeding. I'm about to take you to the hospital." Handsome said, worrying about his sister: She was so stubborn.

"I'm alright, I'm going to change. I don't want to ruin D.J. and Reality's moment. I told you I would be okay. Gigi walked toward the steps, heading to the room she and Honesty shared. She had been bleeding off and on since she went to visit Concrete the first day.

Handsome looked up and saw Killa's nurse. He remembered her telling him that she was a combat nurse in Afghanistan. She could check Gigi out. He walked over to her as she headed toward the door, but his sister was going up the steps.

"Hey, you have a second to check out my sister. She was shot, and now her wound is bleeding." Handsome said to the nurse. This was the first time he had ever been this close to her. She was stunning.

"Sure, I have a minute. Where is she?" Amor said, wondering how she ended up being around so many people who had been victims of crime.

"Sis, Sis, come here right quick and let the nurse check you out." Handsome hollered at the bottom of the stairs, hoping she could hear him over the loudness of the other people.

Gigi turned around and walked back toward her brother. She would do anything except go to the hospital. She hated hospitals.

Amor looked down at her phone. She had just missed a call from Aidan, who had just left. When she looked up, her patient was standing before her. "Beautiful, how did Tristan know I was here?"

Gorgeous replied, "I'm not Beautiful. I'm Gorgeous."

THE END... TO BE CONTINUED